# SWIFT

# SWIFT

## A HISTORICAL NOVEL
## BASED ON A TRUE STORY

## ROBERT A. SHEARER

STEPHEN F. AUSTIN STATE UNIVERSITY PRESS
NACOGDOCHES, TEXAS

Copyright 2014 Robert A. Shearer

Stephen F. Austin State University Press
1936 North Street, LAN 203
Nacogdoches, TX 75962

sfapress@sfasu.edu

LIBRARY OF CONGRESS CATALOGUING-IN-PUBLICATION DATA

Shearer, Robert
Swift: a historical novel/Robert A. Shearer—1st. ed.
p.cm.

ISBN: 978-1-62288-090-4

I. Title

First Edition: 2014

*Dedicated to Skip*

# PREFACE

In December 1941, my parents and I were living peacefully and comfortably in Dallas, Texas. The attack on Pearl Harbor that month changed the lives of millions of Americans. This is a historical account of how murder, mayhem, morbid racism, mental illness, and mobilization for war changed our lives.

Many years later, after my father died, and before she passed away, my mother casually remarked that she and I couldn't leave our small apartment in Bastrop, Texas for three weeks. I was three years old at the time and we lived in Bastrop while my father was an Army officer stationed at Camp Swift, a large Army induction camp.

This story is the product of my research investigating the reason why we couldn't leave the apartment. It is based on a true story and actual events that occurred at the time.

Some of the details are fictional, and all of the names of original characters have been changed, so the story is historical fiction, a murder mystery, a chronicle of a case of military justice, and a case study in mental disturbance occurring prior to the use of sophisticated psychotropic medications to treat mental disturbances.

I had four goals in mind in deciding to write the story. Some of the goals were obvious at the beginning of my writing, and others evolved and emerged as the research progressed. First, I wanted to convey a sense of the chaos, confusion, stress, strain, and fear experienced by people, including my parents, caused by uprooting a diverse population of millions of young people and challenging the traditional social and racial conventions. Second, I wanted to convey an appreciation of the courage, resiliency, and strength of a generation of young people, military and civilian, enduring the hardships of war mobilization.

Third, I wanted to explain, expose, and expel some of the myths, mysteries, and misunderstandings of mental illness by drawing on my lifetime of professional experience in the field. My goal was to further emphasize and reinforce the importance of screening, assessment, diagnosis, and treatment of mental disorders.

Finally, I wanted to communicate the depth of sacrifice, pain, patriotic dedication, resiliency, fear, and courage of the citizens of a small Texas town at a time of war mobilization, civil crisis, criminal victimization, and personal tragedy.

The task of achieving these goals was humbling, challenging, and exciting. Hopefully these goals were achieved and you will enjoy the story.

# Contents

# CHAPTER 1

## BOB-O-LINKS

The massive wall of blue, gray, and greenish clouds stretching across the Northwestern sky foretold the arrival of a "blue norther" in the Dallas area. It looked like the trunk of an ancient tree rolling down a gentle slope, threatening to crush everything in its path. It had raced across the plains of western Texas and Oklahoma. Local residents who had been in the area for several seasons didn't pay too much attention to the approaching storm. This one was late in the season, and it was a big one. So, if you were new to the sight and experience, the storm could be a weather nightmare, or at least, a big surprise.

Some creatures seemed to love the occasion. Hawks and vultures were riding the thermals that arose in front of the cloud wall as it pushed hot air on its march to the southeast. The large birds, with  extended wings, must have been soaring for the pure joy of the experience because they were not gliding  at such heights looking for carrion. They were truly "thunder" birds. The collection of soaring birds looked so calm, distant, and suspended as they looped, circled, and dove through endless patterns in the sky. They seemed unaffected by the flashes of lightening and bursts of thunder chasing them across the plains, but the scene on the ground far below was quite the opposite. Most of the golfers at the Bob-O-Links driving range and "pitch and putt" had been nervously watching the approaching storm for some time. The air was hot, still, and heavy. The only sounds were the "whack-whack-whack" as golfers hit balls off tees and the backdrop of thunder in the distance. As the storm approached, they teed-up at a faster pace because they knew they would have to run for cover in a few minutes. The golfers didn't want to get caught being exposed to lightning out in the open field, but they were anxious to hit all the balls in their buckets and baskets that they had paid for. The white balls that had been driven from the tee boxes littered the green range like hailstones. Many residents of the area had seen the opposite in their yards when hailstones looked like golf balls. In a few minutes, the range would be covered with both hailstones and golf balls.

Bob-O-Links was well outside the residential area and occupied a spot where cotton fields had once covered vast expanses. The entire area east, west, and north of Dallas had been planted in cotton and wheat for over fifty years with fields stretching north to the Red River.

Before the cotton fields, vast prairies of grass covered the black earth north of the city. The grassy prairies were crisscrossed with buffalo trails leading east to a fertile valley along White Rock Creek that was later converted to a lake and water source for the city. The buffalo preferred the lush valley when the grass on the high prairies got dry and sparse and winter winds got colder. The buffalo had been gone from the area for over seventy years, and the city was poised to cover the cotton and wheat fields with urban development. Within ten years or less, the "march of the concrete" would begin, and Bob-O-Links and most of the prairies north of Dallas would disappear.

Golfers on the pitch and put were moving toward the office and parking lot as the storm approached. Art Shafer and Bill Buchan were finishing the seventh hole of the nine-hole course as they watched the sky to the northwest. Art noticed an orange hue on the western end of the cold front which he knew meant the storm was bringing dust from west Texas. Somebody was going to get covered with reddish orange dust or mud along with the other surprises from the storm. They could see the office and carport next to the office at Bob-O-Links, because they had only two holes left to play. They were carrying small golf bags with only two or three clubs, a putter and a couple of pitching wedges. The two men bantered back and forth. Their conversation on the course today was similar to most days when they played—future business and career plans.

"We know this trade area," Buchan said.

"Yea, we both know all of the wholesale grocers in the area and we could be representing a whole line of products, rather than just one," Art added.

"Sure, if we're going to make the trips, we might as well be making more money," Buchan suggested.

"That's a pretty long putt you've got there," he said when he interrupted the conversation.

"Yea, and this green rolls kinda crazy," Art responded.

After a brief silence while he putted, Art continued the conversation.

"Well, Skip and I have talked about having our own brokerage firm someday. I would have to save some money and maybe start with a well established firm and then go out on my own," Art said.

"Where would we get our product lines?" Buchan asked.

"We'd have to go to Atlantic City or Chicago to the Food Brokers Convention, to see if we could land some products. I think we could," Art replied.

"That's how they do it over at old Red Watson's brokerage. One of their salesmen told me that's what they do," Art added.

"I agree and we could do pretty well if this area of Texas continues to grow," Buchan suggested.

"Yes, and most of the big companies are wanting to move into this sales area, so we could be in the right place at the right time," Art speculated.

"By the way, how did you get old man Hosek in Corsicana (Wholesale Grocery) to order half a carload (railroad freight car) of oats? All I could ever get him to order was a half dozen cases of grits," Buchan complained.

"I bribed him," Art shot back with a grin.

"What?" Buchan asked.

"Yea.............sorta," Art hesitated.

"I found out he liked Polish dill pickles, so I took him a case............... well, a case minus one jar. I got the railroad damaged case over at Dallas Wholesale Grocery. One jar was busted and the juice had ruined the labels on the other eleven jars. I cleaned it up a little bit and gave it to him."

"And then he ordered half a carload?" Buchan asked.

"Sure did.................and he loved the pickles," Art added.

"Uh.............um...............um," Buchan mumbled.

The wholesale grocery warehouses had salvage sections devoted to damaged merchandise. On occasion, the railroad would "hump" a freight car. Instead of rolling the car slowly into place to be unloaded into the warehouse, the train engineer would run the mother train a little faster and release the freight car so that it ran down the track and slammed into the stationary cars already positioned to be unloaded.

When "humping" happened, the typical result was damaged merchandise from the sudden and massive shifting of the goods. The opening of the cars got very messy, repulsive, and nauseous when the contents consisted of pickles, syrup, baby food, ketchup, or vinegar. Before the massive metal doors of cars were opened, the various liquid, pungent, and gooey contents would be oozing from the cars and dripping on the ground below the doors. Flying and crawling insects signaled the location of the damaged contents. Two black men, called a "bull gang," assigned to unload the rail car, unloaded the mess. The crushed cargo made their job more difficult, tedious, and nauseating. Now, they had to contend with broken glass and spoiled food.

Bob-O-Links was at the northeast corner of Greenville Avenue and Lovers Lane, across from Luann's Nightclub and Dancehall. The golf complex consisted of small buildings serving as an office or pro shop, storage, and a ball washing area. The balls from the driving range, after they were picked up, were brought in to be washed in discarded wringer washing machines that had the wringers removed. Once they were washed, they were put into buckets and metal baskets in groups of forty or eighty balls for the customers. So, while one man worked in the office, another man, sometimes two, fetched and shagged the balls at night after hours or early in the morning. Then, they washed them for the next afternoon and evening customers. It was difficult to get ball washers and shaggers because the facility was quite far out of town, and the pay was too low for a worker to own an automobile. So, the job was usually taken by someone who rode the streetcar to the end of the line on Abrams Road and then walked a mile or two to the driving range. Workers also had to water and mow the greens of the nine holes which made the job labor intensive and weather dependent. The combination resulted in a less dependable and consistent labor force.

Bob-O-Links was convenient for Art and Bill because they both lived back toward town at the northern edge of the city. They had a lot in common. Both were salesmen for National Oats, reserve military, golfers, and family men. The other thing they had in common, that they couldn't have predicted, was that they both would survive a coming world war with many extraordinary experiences and personal scars. They were both close to thirty years old. As they played the first seven holes, they commented on how it was looking like they were too old to be called into service for the war in Europe. These conversations would change by the time they finished the nine holes of golf.

Art started working for National Oats in Atlanta, Georgia, immediately after graduation from a small liberal arts college in Iowa. The company wanted to expand the sales territory into the Dallas region, so he was transferred to his current sales territory, which included Dallas and most of north and east Texas. His job was to travel to the wholesale grocery warehouses in the area and insure they were stocked with cases of the cylinders of National Oats Brand cereal, so when the retail stores ordered the product it would be available in the warehouse. He also, on occasion, visited the retail stores in the area to make sure they were keeping their shelves fully stocked with all of the oat products.

The job involved extensive travel for the two salesmen from Monday morning to Friday evening, away from their families. Neither of their wives had cars, so it made it tough on the homemakers. The wives had to walk or ride streetcars to get groceries, see a doctor, or take care of other household errands.

"We better get tha hell out of here," Art said.

"Yea, just when I was winning," replied Buchan.

"The wives are alone with the kids. Skip is from Iowa, and she doesn't like these Texas storms."

"I know what you mean. I don't like 'em either."

Both men had seen the destruction tornados could cause. Their travel experiences on the sales trade had brought them into the towns where storms had passed across the landscape of north and east Texas.

"Yea, I saw what was left of Rodessa, Louisana several years ago. It wiped out the town and killed a lot of people," Art said.

"You don't have to twist my arm to get me going," Buchan replied.

Adding to the apprehension, golfers playing behind them began to press them to move on to the eighth hole. Players were getting restless on the entire course, waving their golf clubs in the air to signal for the players ahead of them to hurry.

"What in the hell is going on?" Buchan asked.

"Beats me," Art replied.

The two golfers had looked up from the seventh green, and they could see two men at the office frantically waving their arms. It looked like the course manager, Will Ovard, and the ball washer and general cleanup helper, a man named Radio. Art knew Will fairly well and had visited with him on several occasions when he checked in and paid to play the nine holes.

The other man was different. The man named Radio had seemed strange to Art from the first time he met him. Art could tell Radio was a clean-shaven white man that obviously lived in the streets somewhere in the city, based on the way he dressed and the way he smelled. He was taller than Art, thin, lanky, slightly stooped and pigeon-toed. He usually wore a pair of discarded painter's overalls turned inside out, so all of the paint couldn't be seen. The "high water" pant legs of the overalls were too short and stopped well above his ankles and brogans. The leather shoes were worn so much that the original color, brown or black, had disappeared long ago. He had a strong, musty body odor mixed with the odor of cigarette smoke. His hair looked like it had been cut with hedge clippers, long in some spots and short in others. The helper was older than Art, quite unkempt, and a shy, aloof man. Art would see him at various unusual places around the golf range squatting in the shadows when he wasn't working. Art, who didn't smoke, noticed that he never smiled, seldom spoke, and frequently smoked cigarettes. When he first started playing at Bob-O-Links, Art had made the mistake of asking Radio how he was doing and how he was feeling. It was more of a greeting than an inquiry.

"I've got a bad headache," Radio said.

Art asked him, "How did you get the headache?" He thought he might have been hit by a golf ball since he was on the driving range shagging balls much of the time.

Radio replied, "Somebody put maggots in my ear, and they are eating my brain."

"Who put them in there?" Art asked.

Radio said, "The Dallas Police Department."

"Uh.......um........are you serious?" Art asked.

"Dead serious," Radio replied. Then his face went blank of any emotion, and he started giggling and ran around the corner of the building like a child playing hide-and-seek. He peeked around the corner of the building and then ran away, giggling as he ran.

"Yea................okay............you've got a big problem............ um...........yea..... a problem." Art stammered.

*What tha hell was that? He said maggots? He didn't reply "Fine, how are you." He said maggots............and the police. I wish I hadn't asked the son-of-a-bitch anything. He must have been hit in the head with more than one golf ball. Will must be desperate for workers. This guy is.........is.........is.....different......... scary.*

Based on the man's reply and strange behavior, Art was astounded, dumbfounded, and nervous after a brief conversation. He had never seen a grown man act like a ten year old child.

Art was a salesman, so he was comfortable with starting conversations with strangers. He had learned that "How ya'll doing? Hi ya'll, and Where ya'll from?" were universal greetings from Georgia to Texas. His job required the skill, and he took pride in his conversation skills. The man didn't seem, to Art, to be particularly dangerous or violent. He was almost the opposite. He seemed shy, aloof, and withdrawn. He never smiled or acknowledged others and seemed to move robotically through his tasks, but he was always alert. His dark eyes caught a glimpse of everything going on around him. He didn't miss anything, and he didn't have the "shy eye" that Art had seen in people who never looked at you or were always looking down to avoid eye contact. On another occasion, Art noticed the man was giggling and grimacing for no apparent reason. He had also seen Radio wearing several layers of clothing when the temperature didn't seem to suggest the need for so much clothing. Art guessed he was poor and slept in the street, but he had a quick mind. Art noticed that he worked hard and got along well with Will. He just said some very odd things. Art was correct about Radio getting hit by golf balls. He had been hit many times. On nights when the range was busy, Will would run out of golf balls, and Radio would have to go out on the range to replenish the supply. Sometimes the golfers would intentionally try to hit him, so whether it was intentional or accidental, he had been hit by the white flying missiles. Ever since the encounter, Art had been very uneasy, and he steered clear of the man whenever he came to Bob-O-Links. Besides, he had seen a lot of men like him working in the grocery warehouses in the region he traveled. So, he didn't pay a lot of attention to the man who had given him the heebie-jeebies.

The helper was one of those rare, mysterious, misunderstood, eternally mistreated, and handicapped individuals who experience vivid dreams, voices, or noises when he was awake. Art was correct in his suspicions that the man was crazy and a street bum, but he didn't know where he went when he wasn't working at the golf course. Sometimes he would be working when he came to play the course, and sometimes he wouldn't. Art surmised the man must have traveled from somewhere downtown on the streetcar.

Radio looked like he'd slept in his clothes and was generally unkempt, but he had the "white privilege" advantage because, even though he was poor, he was a white man. This meant Radio could go many places and do many things colored men couldn't do.

In addition to picking up and washing golf balls, Radio had additional job duties. He mowed the grass on the driving range with a push mower, swept off the tee boxes, picked up all of the broken tees, cleaned up all of the trash left from the previous day, cleaned and stacked the "loaner" golf clubs, and watered the grass. He had to be very careful about when he got on the driving range to mow and water, because the men sometimes deliberately tried to hit him with the balls they were driving off the tees. It wasn't easy for Will to find a day laborer who would work at the Bob-O-Links location, so Radio was fairly secure in his job, with very little competition for his employment.

Colored men wouldn't be working at Bob-O-Links because it was too far from town for a colored man to risk getting home before darkness fell. There was a universal rule that colored men were not to be seen in the white areas of town after the sun went down. Bob-O-Links required evening and night work. Radio seemed to be one of the few men available because he could move freely around the city at any time, night or day.

The universal rule didn't apply to colored women who could move freely about the city at all hours working as maids, cooks, nannies, and housekeepers. They filled the streetcars in the mornings on the way to white areas of town and in the evenings returned to the colored sections of town. Regardless of the direction, the colored women always sat in the back of the streetcar. If a colored woman didn't get off somewhere along the line and rode the car to the end of the line, she would simply get up from her seat and walk to the other end of the streetcar as the conductor flipped the seats for travel in the opposite direction. The conductor also took down the electrical arm that contacted the overhead lines on one end of the car and raised the arm on the other end of the car. His final act before going back in the opposite direction was to flip over all of the small signs above each seat that said "white" on one side and "colored" on the other side with arrows pointing toward the rear of the streetcar on the "colored" side and toward the front on the "white" side. Furthermore, all white people knew who "colored" referred to even though most never used the word to refer to black people. The arrows seemed unneeded because everybody knew the expected seating rules.

Skip's younger brother, John, had visited them the previous summer. He had traveled by train, alone, to Dallas at age twelve to stay with Art and Skip. He soon discovered the streetcar lines in Dallas that he had never seen in a small town in Iowa. He would board the streetcar on Abrams Road, ride it downtown, to the end of the line in all directions, back to downtown and back to the end of the line on Abrams Road. So, the streetcars were a vital transportation artery for people who had fifteen cents to travel around Dallas for work or recreation.

Art knew very little about the background of the man they called Radio. But, the most unmistakable thing about the man was the appearance of his teeth. Radio had a deep horizontal groove across the face of his upper and lower teeth. Poor dental hygiene and cigarette staining caused the groove to be dark and dirty consequently Radio rarely smiled so as not to show the horror of his mouth. The groove was the unmistakable mark of a child born to a mother who had syphilis during her pregnancy. Art had seen the cosmetic nightmare on a man when he worked in the steel mills in Ohio as a teenager. Then, and now, it was disgusting and grotesque. Art assumed the condition was caused by poor dental hygiene.

Even though he had seen the worker at the golf course three or four times, Art knew he was a strange, confusing, and unusual character, so seeing the two men frantically waving their arms to get his attention meant something serious had happened. He dreaded that something had happened to Skip or his three year old son.

*Had somebody phoned the golf course with bad news?*

*Had somebody seen a tornado coming?*

*Was somebody hurt or injured?*

When Art and Buchan got to the ninth hole, Will ran over to them and excitedly said the Japanese had bombed Pearl Harbor. Art turned to Buchan and said:

"The Japs bombed Pearl Harbor."

"Oh shit," Buchan said. "I bet we kicked their asses. Where tha hell is Pearl Harbor?"

"Beats me." Art replied.

*Why is he asking me? He's in the Navy. I don't think we covered Pearl Harbor in ROTC. It's probably some godforsaken outpost that nobody ever heard of.*

The two men looked at each other and then Buchan said, "Looks like I'm in the Navy."

"See ya later. I'm gonna call Skip," Art declared.

"Yea, I'll call when you get through," Buchan added.

"Okay, I'll see ya Monday morning," Art signed off.

It was a Sunday in December, 1941, and the storm was racing across the golf course. Paper, white dust, and debris was swirling high in the air, driven by dust devils that could be easily seen across the open fields. The swirling cylinders looked like they were made of baby powder as they picked up the white dust in the parking lot.

The temperature was dropping, and the men could hear large raindrops hitting the metal roof on the storage building. All of the other golfers were dashing for their cars and pitching golf clubs into the trunks of their vehicles. None of the golfers wanted to be caught in the open when lightning started cracking. They could see the flashes a few miles to the northwest.

The line of black, brown, and dark green coupes and sedans, nosed-in side-by-side, began to scramble in the parking lot, as they also kicked up clouds of white dust, a road-surfacing product of the white rock quarries in the area. The subterranean white rock played an important role in the development of the entire north and east Dallas region because the rich, black gumbo, called "black waxy," was excellent for cotton production, but useless for road surfaces. Unfortunately, when the black dirt got wet, it was impossible for cars, trucks, tractors, or construction vehicles to navigate. They quickly got stuck. When it was extremely dry or wet, farmers couldn't dig holes for fence posts by hand or by power augers. When it got wet, cattle in feed lots had to be pulled out by ropes from hip deep mud before they developed hoof rot. When it got extremely dry, a variety of farm animals could break a leg or ankle in the six inch cracks in the earth.

The crushed, white rock helped open the area for development by making roads that were passable in wet weather. The quarry pits dotted the "White Rock" region like brilliant white craters. One of the pits was converted, after the war, into the Devils Speedway stock car racetrack. Art took his children there several times many years after the war.

Art threw his clubs in the back of his Dodge coupe and ran to use the phone at the office. He wanted to call Skip so she wouldn't worry too much. She was only twenty-one years old. She had a small child and a husband that was most certainly going off to war.

"Did you hear the news?" he asked.

"Yes," she replied in a very quiet voice. "It just came over the radio and the president just declared war."

"We'll have to sell the golf clubs and shotguns," he added.

Skip didn't say much because she knew what the news meant when she heard the radio broadcast. It meant their lives were going to be turned upside down along with the aching possibility she could lose her new husband.

"I'll be there in a minute. It's getting pretty rough here with this storm blowing in."

"Okay, I've got everything in the house."

Skip had run in from the backyard where she had been quickly snatching the clothes off the line as the clothespins flipped off the clothes in all directions. When Art called, she was a little out of breath from the rush of getting lawn chairs, toys, and clothes out of the strong wind. In his job as a salesman, Art wore business attire. This requirement meant he wore a coat, tie, and dress shirt in the Texas heat. And, since cars, homes, offices, and warehouses weren't air conditioned, he went through a lot of dress shirts. Skip washed, air dried, and ironed  many  dress shirts. The clothes line had been filled with dress shirts hanging close to the ground and drying in the sun before the storm arrived.

Art shifted the 1941 Dodge Luxury Liner coupe into gear and headed back toward the city. The temperature was dropping and the raindrops were pelting the trunk of the coupe. He was driving quite fast, but the thoughts in his mind were racing faster and bouncing around his mind.

*Second lieutenant in the Army reserve. No military training since ROTC in college. No more job!.............War!........... Where would the family go?.............damned storm is getting worse.*

He could barely see the road ahead from the rain now blowing in sheets across the open fields.

The European war with Germany was raging and everybody who followed the news knew it could get worse.

*But, the Japs....................the goddamned crazy Japs just started a war.*

"Shit!" he said.

The coupe had hit a deep stretch of water and lurched to the left.

"Shit!"

He wasn't too worried about the deepening water. The coupe was heavy and it had big tires. That characteristic, combined with his experience of traveling four or five days a week as a salesman in many storms, gave him confidence he could plow his way through this storm. Marble sized hail started pelting the coupe and it sounded like rocks hitting the car's metal top and glass back window. He kept the Dodge in second gear.

"Shit!"

*Now the bastards will want me. They didn't want me before, but now they will.*

The Dodge coupe was taking a pelting, but it was like an Army tank and kept on rolling quickly down Greenville Avenue toward the one story, small, white, frame house on Somerville Street that Art and Skip had rented.

When he left the house earlier in the day, he was dressed for warm weather, but now he could feel the temperature had dropped several degrees as the front passed the area. The hail was building up in small drifts along the roadside, and he could hear it crunching and cracking under the wheels of the Dodge.

When he thought about going to war, he got a chill because he hadn't thought about anything military for over three years. He had been the ROTC cadet commander at a small college in Iowa where he graduated. He was planning a military career and was excited about his future in the military, but since the country had been at peace, he really had not been planning to go to war. He had grown up during the great depression and attended college by working part-time at several jobs.

*Am I going to fight the Japs or Germans? What will I do with the family? I really don't know a damned thing about killing people. How quickly is all of this going to happen? How much will the military pay be? Will Skip follow me from place to place?*

The weather was getting colder, but what really gave him chills were the memories of ROTC in college. It was more like a military club than combat military training. It mostly consisted of "drill and ceremonies." In reality, the cadets spent a lot of time on the parade field marching, passing-in-review, and standing for inspection. The appearance of a cadet's uniform was an all-consuming preoccupation. Brass was polished. Shoes were shined. Ties were tied with a specific knot and at a specific length. Inspections of the cadets were regularly conducted. Discipline and appearance were stressed, admired, and rewarded. He didn't remember discussing the subject of killing people, getting killed, or getting wounded, but he became very experienced in barking out close order drill orders: "order, ARMS; parade, REST; forward, MARCH; by the right flank, MARCH; about, FACE; rear, MARCH; double time, MARCH; right shoulder, ARMS; and port, ARMS."

He was a member of the rifle team, but never fired a high caliber rifle, only 22 caliber target rifles. The only military rifles they had were for drill purposes, and they had the firing pins removed. Many of them had stocks that had suffered from dry rot, so many had broken stocks. They were vintage World War l, bolt-action Springfield rifles. Most of the instructors were World War l veterans, some of whom never had been in combat.

The poor condition of military training was the result of military downsizing during the depression, because some influential people were convinced World War l was the last world war to ever be fought. This attitude, along with a political sentiment of isolation, led to a crisis in the military of few officers, scarce and outdated equipment, and a lack of interest in the nation in anything military when war was declared in 1941.

When he graduated, he was given a reserve commission. This meant he would not be on active duty in the Army; his career was sidetracked, and he would have to get a civilian job. He had put a lot of time and effort into ROTC. He took military classes, drilled cadets on the drill field during the week, reviewed the cadets early in the morning on Wednesdays, shot on the rifle team, and was elected to a select club known as the "Scabbard and Blade." He worked through the ranks and was promoted to the position of Cadet Commander of the Corp. It all seemed like great fun at the time and in the distant past, but now he realized he was very unprepared to go into combat as an officer. Perhaps, he realized, now he would get some practical, realistic, and modern combat military training.

His anxiety turned to anger when he recalled why he was given a reserve commission. The night before he was scheduled to take his physical exam, he went to a party after the military ball, where he had escorted Skip, and consumed some gin whiskey. The next day when he took the physical exam he showed to have blood in his urine. He flunked the physical. He couldn't be sure, but it was probably the gin he drank.

In the back of his mind, he had always suspected it may have been the case—they just didn't need any more officers at the time. It seemed like a weak excuse to refuse a cadet with his credentials.

Whatever it was, it was the reason he was in the present mess of having to completely change his life. Furthermore, he would be behind in rank compared to his former peers who had gone on active duty. By this time, they would have been promoted to captains, majors, and higher. He was a Second Lieutenant so most of them would be his superiors in rank because it was easier and quicker to be promoted if you were on active duty.

When he steered the Dodge into the driveway of the house they rented, he had an unusual and unexpected thought cross his mind.

*Where would the crazy ball washer at Bob-O-Links be spending this upcoming cold and rainy night?*

The thought left him quickly when the reality of his current situation returned and consumed his thoughts. All future business and personal plans were suspended with one radio broadcast. Art and Skip spent the first evening, after the news of the bombing, deciding what items they owned should be thrown away, sold, shipped to Georgia, or taken in the Dodge. They shipped the furniture, because they had a moving allowance. The golf clubs and shotguns were sold. Before they left, they took family pictures in front of the little, white, frame house on Somerville Street.

It wasn't long before the letter Art expected came from the Department of the Army. It was addressed to 2nd Lt. Arthur Leo Shafer. It indicated that he was to report to Ft. Benning, Georgia within sixty days for combat infantry school. The family moved to Columbus, Georgia in March, 1942, and Art started training at Ft. Benning. Art and Skip enjoyed living in Dallas. They were comfortable. Art had a good job, and the family had settled into a routine. They hoped to return someday, after the war, to the sunny and warm climate of Dallas. Deep in their hearts, they knew the war could easily take them far from Dallas, and they might never return. Now they had to uproot again and move back to Georgia where the family had resided just three years earlier. Skip wrote a letter to her younger brother to tell him he wouldn't be able to visit the next summer. She also wrote a letter to her mother in Iowa to inquire about her father's health. He had traveled to Rochester, Minnesota several times to be treated for cancer.

She was very worried, along with the rest of the family, because the primary treatment for cancer was surgery to remove the cancerous tissue. He had to go back several times because they didn't get all of it, and the cancer returned. It returned and returned again.

# Chapter 2

## Radio

The rainwater pouring off the narrow eave of the building blew against the gray weathered clapboards and dropped in a sheet on the coal oil soaked tarp. The water hitting the stiff tarp made a sound like marbles bouncing on a tabletop. Radio had pulled the tarp over himself sometime after midnight, probably around three o'clock in the morning. It was a large truck tarp so, most of it was covering him, but part of it was out in the rain. He had crawled under the back of an abandoned building on Deep Elm (or Ellum) to sleep somewhere warm and dry with protection from the storm.

Deep Elm was the shanty town or skid row section of Dallas. It was the place where Radio had spent most of his life. During his life, many shady or questionable enterprises had come and gone on Deep Elm, and he was a known but unnoticed regular resident. Deep Elm consisted of Central Avenue which was located perpendicular to Elm Street and parallel to the Houston and Central Texas railroad tracks. On Deep Elm, there were pawn shops, tattoo studios, domino halls, Chinese laundries, bawdy houses, whorehouses, boarding houses, and pool halls. On the crowded sidewalks, drug dealers, crap shooters, card sharks, hustlers, and pimps loitered day and night. Cheap whiskey, cocaine, or marijuana could be purchased about any time. Since the 1900s, Deep Elm had been populated by African-Americans and European immigrants. In the 1920s, it became a popular community for jazz and blues musicians. Blind Lemon Jefferson, Leadbelly, Texas Bill Day, Lightning Hopkins, and Bessie Smith all performed in Deep Elm. At one time, there were a dozen nightclubs, cafes, and domino parlors in Deep Elm. By the 1940s, Deep Elm had become a rough, violent, and dangerous place. Most of the clubs and businesses were closed or boarded up. Deep Elm had evolved into a haven and hideout for more violent individuals. The community now consisted of transient thieves, predatory thugs, and threatening street toads. They lived in, around, and under the vacant, dilapidated, and unpainted buildings. Most of Radio's acquaintances were gone, and the once colorful community had died now that the economic conditions in Dallas had gotten better and immigrants had moved on. The community had changed for the worse and he was still stuck in Deep Elm with nowhere to go. He was just trying to stay alive in his theater of cruelty.

Radio had survived on Deep Elm by hustling odd jobs or stealing and then pawning or selling the stolen items. When he walked through the avenues where the wealthier people lived, he occasionally could find a musical instrument left by a careless child who lived in the large two story mansions. He would sell it at a pawn shop or second hand store on Deep Elm. He also caddied at the golf courses around the city. Most of the caddies were colored men, but he could usually get a bag to carry if he arrived at the caddy stand early enough. His primary job though was helping and shagging golf balls at Bob-O-Links golf course when the weather was suitable for golfing. The day before, the weather had been perfect for golfing, so he had gone to Bob-O-Links to work, but the cold and wet weather had forced him to return to Deep Elm.

He was known around Deep Elm as Radio. The name started when he was younger. He told people that the radios were sending him messages, so when people saw him on the street they would make fun of him and point to the nearest radio. The name stuck and it was doubtful that anybody knew his real name, who he was, or where he came from. In any case, in 1941, Deep Elm could be a dangerous place, but he knew how to survive and take care of himself.

In addition to Radio, Deep Elm was a haven for other socially marginal individuals. They weren't actually his friends, but would have been more accurately described as acquaintances. They weren't friends because they drifted in and out of Deep Elm, disappearing for days, weeks, months, or even years and then reappearing after an absence. The continually changing social group could be seen squatting or standing in alleys, drinking wine, or consuming other mysterious substances, or standing around a burn-barrel for warmth in the wintertime. Strangers also drifted to Deep Elm, left, and then never returned, but some of the regular characters included the following:

"Rhino" came from the Reinhardt community northeast of Dallas. He traveled up and down Dixon's Branch, and his appearance looked like he lived in a creek. His clothes were held together with rope and twine. When times were hard and food scarce, he caught, cooked, and ate fish, crawfish, and turtles in the creek. In some places, Dixon's Branch had carved small, deep, and narrow canyons through the rich black top layer of earth, and into the white rock layer beneath the black earth. In dry months, clear, deep, and isolated pools of water were left in the creek. The food supply was trapped in the pools up and down the creek. In several places along the creek, rib bones of a prehistoric bison could be seen protruding from the walls of the creek at the point where the black dirt layer met the white rock layer. The rib bones signaled that a bison had been killed and butchered on the spot by Native Americans thousands of years earlier. The abandoned carcass had been buried by the shifting black earth being blown and washed over the years. Dixon's Branch was Rhino's natural avenue to Dallas, and he made it his home when the stream wasn't filled with a raging torrent of muddy water from heavy rain in the Reinhardt region;

"Gimp" was reportedly from Poetry, Texas, near Terrell, Texas. When it existed, long before the prohibition of alcoholic beverages, the town consisted of only saloons. The man walked with a limp that was the result of a wound received in a bar room fight in one of the saloons and from the pervasive arthritis in his joints that was a result of being a hod carrier most of his life in Dallas;

"Greaser" was from Pecan Gap, Texas and he got his nickname from his use of axle grease in his hair. His specialty was illegally riding freight trains in and out of Dallas. Most drifters wouldn't risk riding on the trains because they could either be beaten up by train bosses or they could get killed by shifting cargo in the train cars. There were many gruesome stories told, and no doubt embellished, on Deep Elm about men being cut in half or crushed while they were illegally "hopping a freight;"

"Smooth" was given his name because he didn't have any teeth. His true name was Ochie Milltop, and he sometimes lived in Farmers Branch. Not having teeth was quite common for poor people who couldn't afford false teeth, which were expensive. Dental hygiene was uncommon for wealthy citizens and nonexistent for poor people. "Smoothe" rarely spoke. Instead, he communicated by blowing a military style whistle. He had a pattern of communication that everyone seemed to understand. "Hello" was represented by one tweet on the whistle. "How are you today?" was answered by three blasts on the whistle. When "Smoothe" was happy, he would raise one arm in the air and produce a continuous whistling sound. When he was unhappy, he produced a low clicking sound on the whistle or a low pitched ratatattat. People in Deep Elm said they had heard him speak, but Radio had never seen him without the whistle in his mouth.

"Low life" was from Crisp, Texas, south of Dallas. He had spent most of his life as a laborer in the brick factories south of Dallas in Palmer, Ferris, Crisp, and Groesbeck, Texas. His thumbs and most of his fingers were missing from work related accidents. They had been crushed over time by loads of bricks slipping and hitting them.;

"Freeg" was a man who was a descendent of one of the settlers of the French commune, La Reunion, that had been established in 1855 on the banks of the Trinity River. His true name was either DuFreeg or DeFreeg, but most people just called him "Freeg." He was addicted to cheap wine, like many other bums, vagrants, or drifters in Deep Elm. The most popular brands were Ripple, Night Train, and Thunderbird. A radio commercial at the time broadcast:

"What's the word?

Thunderbird.

How's it sold?

Good and cold.

What's the jive?

Bird's alive.

What's the price?

Thirty twice."

It was easy to tell who had been drinking Thunderbird or other cheap wines. The concoctions turned their lips and mouths black. It made the bums and winos look like they had been chewing a lump of charcoal. The cheap wines were manufactured and marketed right after the repeal of prohibition to capture the skid row market.

As late as the 1950's, the popular radio jingle was a part of the inter-personal communication of many young people of Dallas. On one level, it became a common greeting of "What's the word?" On another level, it became a popular nightclub and drinking chant. Someone in a crowd would yell "What's the word?" and another person or the whole crowd would respond with "Thunderbird." The popularity of the greeting faded by the 1960s when a new generation of hip young people emerged. "Freeg" was seriously addicted to cheap wines and he could be seen frequently passed out in a ditch or alley. He was killed, while Radio lived on Deep Elm, by a train that ran over him after he passed out on the tracks;

"Old Red" was a light skinned black man who gave advice and told fortunes. Light skinned black people or people of Native American-Black mixture were frequently referred to as "Red" or "High yeller." He was a very influential, respected, and powerful individual that was largely unnoticed in Dallas. Many wealthy and influential white people in Dallas sought his advice and counsel. "Old Red" was careful to keep his connections and "clients" confidential and anonymous and his business discreet. He drifted between Dallas and Mineola, Texas, giving advice to white people on a wide variety of personal problems, dilemmas, and conflicts. He had to be very wary, cautious, and elusive because his business carried a high risk of racial hatred and violence, as it was for any black person with power and influence. Very light skinned black people, who could pass as white, frequently experienced more of the venom of white racists. Unsuspecting white people would lower any inhibitions they had and feel safer to tell racist jokes, use racist language, or direct racial slurs that they may have been less likely to do around more conspicuously appearing black people. Unfortunately, for some white people, it didn't make any difference who was present. For "Old Red," there were very real advantages and disadvantages in being light skinned;

"River Rat" had worked on steamboats when they briefly had traveled on the Trinity River. He had also worked on crews dynamiting log jams or "snags" in the river to clear for steamboats to operate on the river. As a result of an accident, he lost an eye and was badly disfigured on one side of his face. A chunk of wood thrown from an explosion had hit him in the head;

"Jimma" was the resident of Deep Elm that knew Radio the best. The man was a World War One veteran who had been disfigured in a mustard gas attack while he was in combat in France. He had burn scars on his face and hands. He only spoke with a whisper because the deadly gas had stripped the mucous membranes of his vocal chords and esophagus. In addition to his disfigurement, he limped with occasional shaking, tremors, and muscle contractions as a result of shell shock in the war. He was treated in a French hospital by being shocked with electric cattle prods in an attempt to stop the tremors. The tremors didn't stop. The man worked at the state fair grounds cleaning animal dung from the show pens. Radio saw him on a regular basis when the two rode the trolley together out to the fair grounds;

"Eboo Ease" was a black man that worked in a shoe shine parlor in Deep Elm. Radio didn't know his whole or real name. Some people called him "Unk." He had grown up on a sharecropper farm in Lancaster, Texas. Radio liked to sit on the steps of the shine parlor and listen to "Eboo" because the man always knew the latest gossip and stories that were circulating around Dallas and Deep Elm. The strange social relationship arrangement allowed black people to be friendly and almost equal to Radio in Deep Elm, but not in the rest of the city. Conversely, Radio avoided black people in the rest of the city. It seemed to be okay for outcasts, second class citizens, and minority groups to mingle as long as it was confined to Deep Elm. The obvious manifestation of this was black and white businesses existing side by side, an arrangement that would not be tolerated outside of Deep Elm;

Finally, an additional acquaintance of Radio's wasn't exactly an acquaintance because in all of the years that Radio spent on Deep Elm, he was never certain that the man was a real person. His name was Mobeety Munson. Some people referred to him as "Mobe," "Old Mo," or "Beety." The paradox of Mobeety was that everybody on Deep Elm knew his name for years, but nobody was quite sure that anybody had ever seen him, at least not in human form. He was a mythical character and his karma, bad and good, was legendary. Like other residents, Radio was fascinated with the illusive man. He spoke as if he knew him on a personal basis. He told people he had seen and talked to Mobeety on a regular basis. For Radio, he was a real person and he liked the notion that he knew something that few others knew. He knew Mobeety. As he got older, Mobeety became his close advisor, relative, and confidant. Like other residents, Radio was also superstitious, suggestible, and intrigued by ghost stories and urban legends. The legend of Mobeety Munson seemed to flower during the hard times of the Great Depression in Dallas, and be forgotten after World War II. Some people said he came from Shreveport, Lousiana or Preston's Crossing on the Red River. Whatever the case, he seemed to be a doppelganger or a person with a ghostly counterpart. Sometime he was seen as a person and other times as an apparition. He had been seen in the Turtle Creek area, near Doran's Point, in the Nussbaumer community, and under the Houston Street viaduct. He had an uncanny knack for outwitting the cops and railroad detectives. He would mysteriously appear in back alley crap games and then disappear. He was mostly known on Deep Elm as a card shark, crap shooter, and an overall slippery character.

The most fascinating aspect of Mobeety was that residents of Deep Elm would refer to him enviously and admiringly as if he was a wise hero, sage, or oracle. They would say:

"Old Mo would have.............;" or

"Beety told me....................;" or

"Sounds like Mobeety's been in the area...............;" or

"Mobeety struck again."

When residents referred to him in a positive manner, they usually used the names "Mo" or "Mobe." When they referred to one of his negative ghostly interventions, they would, usually use the name "Beety." So, if a building burned in the area, they would say "Beety" probably did it, meaning the mythological character had set the fire.

There were many stories about Mobeety's adventures. One story related that he survived a massive flood on the Trinity River by clinging to a large log. He rode it all the way to Eagle Ford to escape perishing in the flooded river.

The origin of the Mobeety legend was unknown. The fact that he had a first and last name indicates there was probably, at one time, an actual person in the area, but time, imagination, embellishment, and fantasy had erased the specifics of his past. The most popular explanation was that his grave wasn't moved when White Rock Lake was constructed. His resting place was overlooked in the disinterment of graves projected to be covered by water. His grave was either underwater or under the earthen dam.

The legend placed his ghost wandering the downtown streets of Dallas looking for the officials responsible for the error and oversight. Whatever the case, like other residents, Radio thought he knew the man well enough to be considered a close friend.

How was Radio seen by the residents of Deep Elm? His acquaintances knew Radio to have two personalities. The first personality consisted of a general street bum, homeless man, and drifter, so he didn't seem to be any different than many other residents. The second personality emerged occasionally when Radio had "spells" of silliness, immaturity, and other odd behaviors. He laughed and grimaced at unexpected times and became angry just as unpredictably. Most residents suspected that something wasn't quite right with Radio, but it was Deep Elm and there were many unusual people who came through the community, particularly mentally and emotionally challenged individuals.

Most of Radio's acquaintances drifted back and forth between Deep Elm and small farm communities around Dallas, like Scyene, Farmers Branch, or Garland. Some came from "Hells Half Acre" in Fort Worth, Texas, an area similar to Deep Elm in the city west of Dallas. Most men were poor, handicapped, or both. They came to Deep Elm because of local rejection in the small conservative towns, self banishment, or a combination of both reasons. When they were in Dallas, they had to avoid serious contact with Dallas police, and when they didn't, they would flee to one of the small towns where law enforcement was not as concentrated and prevalent. Most had physical deformities, emotional handicaps, or addiction problems. Others were simply poor, homeless, or unlucky.

In many cases, they came to Dallas because it was "wet" which meant that liquor, beer, and wine were sold and legal to consume. Most of the counties north and east of the city were "dry." The dividing line between "wet" and "dry" was the meandering course of White Rock Creek. Bootleg liquor was expensive in the "dry" areas of East and North Texas. "Moonshine" whiskey was also available, but it could kill you if you drank a lethal concoction. So, the attraction was cheap wine that was available in Deep Elm. The "proper" white citizens of Dallas viewed Deep Elm with an uncomfortable anxiety and fear, mixed with curiosity and exotic imagination. They were ambivalent about the freewheeling and free living lifestyle they imagined that existed in Deep Elm. They were envious of the lifestyle and, at the same time, disgusted with the sin, evil, crime, and decadence they imagined about Deep Elm. At its zenith, the Deep Elm mythology ranged from romanticism to disgust and revulsion. Most white citizens wished Deep Elm would disappear, but they would drive across town to show the area to visitors, much in the same way they did when the "red light" districts had existed at an earlier time in the history of Dallas. Deep Elm also contributed to the consumption of beer and wine by more affluent white teenagers. The legally underage consumers would drive to the "wet" areas in and around Deep Elm to purchase alcohol. A car load of kids would park next to or behind a liquor store and wait for a passing adult, who they would offer money to make a straw purchase. Deep Elm had an influence far beyond the physical and social perimeter of the community, especially when the underage drinkers drank too much and got into trouble back in the white areas of the city.

The building Radio had crawled under was abandoned, but he heard voices in the room above whispering about him. He heard people whispering about him frequently and they were doing it again. He couldn't tell exactly what they were saying, but he knew they were talking about him.

The tarp still had an intense smell, because it had been soaked in coal oil. The area under the building smelled of feces and urine left by vagrants and winos that used the outdoor facilities to relieve themselves. Radio thought the floor of the building above smelled like mustard. It wasn't a faint smell, but one that burned his nostrils and made him uncomfortable.

Even though he was under the tarp beneath the building, he was still very cold because the cold air behind the storm from the night before had blown through Deep Elm. He was in pain over most of his body, and when he moved the pain got worse. His legs and back were bruised and stiff. His face was swollen, and his chest hurt when he took a deep breath. He had fallen asleep, but the pain and cold woke him up.

He had made a painful and almost deadly mistake on the way home from work. He got off the streetcar, after work, to buy some cigarettes at Harrells drug store in Lakewood. The streetcar went through Lakewood, passing in front of the drugstore. He knew it was a big risk because a local gang controlled the area. From his view at the front of the streetcar, everything looked quiet around the store, so he took a chance and got off the streetcar. He went in and got the cigarettes. When he came out of the store, he had to wait about fifteen minutes for the next streetcar to come by the store. That's when seven or eight young gang members caught him and pushed him along the sidewalk and around the corner of the building. He guessed they were some of the members of the Lakewood Rats gang. He knew there were two notorious gangs in Dallas, the Lakewood Rats and the Frogtown Rats. The Frogtown gang controlled the west side of Dallas; the Lakewood gang claimed the north side. Radio had avoided going to the west side of town to avoid the Frogtown gang, but the Lakewood Rats had him now.

"Hey wino, what are you doing in this part of town?" one of the Rats asked.

"I was.........," Radio tried to reply.

"You're a damn queer," another Rat interrupted.

"Yea, you're a gawddammed low-life. That's what you are," another said as the group started pushing and shoving him around behind Harrells.

Radio knew about the Rats, and he knew he was in serious trouble. He could get beat-up or even killed. He knew fighting back was useless. There were too many of them, and they smelled like they had been drinking beer. He was scared and got more worried as they continued to push him around.

That's when they really got agitated and let-loose on him. They were used to gang fights and only respected an aggressive combative encounter. It looked to the gang members that this guy wasn't going to fight back, so they were going to punish his weakness, have a lot of fun, and release a lot of pent-up hostility at his expense. They had done it before and frequently boasted about "rolling" winos, beating-up queers, and driving around throwing cabbage heads at colored people.

"The fucker's yellow," one of the Rats screamed.

"Yea, he's a bastard and a low-life bum," said another.

The gang members were now jumping around in an excited frenzy, each hoping to get in as many "licks" to this guy as they could. They were cussing and punching the air in mock attacks in predatory anticipation.

"What's wrong wino? Are you yellow?" a gang member asked.

The group tightened the circle around Radio as they prepared to "work him over."

"We're going to kill you, you son of a bitch," several Rats started chanting.

They had started by pushing him around, but now they were hitting him in the head and stomach. He finally slumped to the ground, and the group screamed with delight. Once on the ground, they started kicking him as he curled-up in a fetal position for protection from the painful blows to his body.

"Let's kill the bastard," one of the Rats said.

"Yea! Yea! Let's kill 'em," chimed several others.

The beating went on and on, and Radio could tell for sure the group had been drinking beer. The group got more agitated. One of them would run at him and kick him, and the rest would cheer loudly and splash beer on him.

"Have a drink wino," they would say laughingly.

When he thought the beating wouldn't end and he couldn't take any more, he looked up at the night sky and wailed.

"Ma, they're going to kill me."

"Ma!...........Ma!..............," he said as he went in and out of consciousness.

The Rats were in an excited and drunken frenzy, and they weren't going to stop torturing the bruised body on the ground.

Suddenly, Radio heard one of the Rats, undoubtedly the leader, tell the others:

"Throw his ass in the car and let's get out of here."

He was relieved the beating had stopped, and glad they hadn't used a bicycle chain on him. He had seen the gruesome results of the chains used on men in Deep Elm that gang members had attacked. So, most street people were terrified of being caught and hit with the chains. His relief was still overshadowed by the fear that they weren't going to let him go.

Four of the Rats drug him to one of their cars and shoved him into the back seat as all of the gang members started cars and drove off in a caravan. In the back seat, the twelve year old girl's voice screamed at him again as it had in the past.

*You're a bastard. You're evil. Your mother is a whore. You're possessed by the devil and you're brain is diseased. This is your punishment.*

The little girl always screamed at him when he got nervous, frightened, or when a situation got out of his control. The screaming episodes were relentless, piercing, and had begun when he was a teenager. He had heard preachers on the street and in the missions of Deep Elm talk about the devil, so he thought the voices could be the devil talking to him. He became more sure of it as he got older. He couldn't figure out any other reason for the torment and why his current misery was occurring. During some of his lowest moments on Deep Elm, he frequently asked himself, "Why is this happening to me, why is my life like this, and why am I being punished?" He was asking these questions now.

He was in the car for only a short distance before the driver stopped the car on a dirt road surrounded by tall grass. They forced him down a well-worn path to a clearing under the Santa Fe Railroad trestle where the railroad crossed over White Rock Creek. Some of the Rats had gotten to the location ahead of the group he was with, and they had a small fire burning on the dry ground under the trestle. The clearing under the trestle was a popular, but secluded location on the bank of the creek.

They shoved Radio on the ground and proceeded to have a drunken discussion about what to do with him. They were whooping and hollering in an excited frenzy of alcohol driven anger and emotional release.

"Let's roast the turd," one voice yelled.

"No, let's corn-hole him," another Rat suggested as the group broke into screams of delight.

"Let's cut his nuts off," another voice added.

The macabre and potentially lethal deliberations persisted for at least thirty minutes while Radio lay on the dry ground near the fire. As he cowered on the dry creek bank, he looked up and saw the light from the fire flickering on the beams and cross members of the underside of the trestle. This looked to him like the hell the preachers had talked about.

He heard one of the Rats suggest, "Let's devil the bastard."

Others replied, "Yes, yes, yes!"

A couple said "No!" and a brief chicken-fight erupted which consisted of the participants dancing around and throwing mock punches. Rats were lobbying to "Devil" him. Others were screaming for something more drastic. Still others were too drunk to know what was happening. And, some were verbally fighting about what to do next. The melee had been in full blossom for about ten minutes when one of the sub-leaders appeared from the dark path. He was carrying a can of paint. He told two of the Rats that were still sober to get Radio up, and then four of them held him up in a crucifix position and stripped-off his clothes. Radio was too groggy and confused to do or say anything. To the delight of the rest of the gang, two of the Rats started painting him with red barn paint. They painted his face and hair and the rest of his body. When they painted his genitals, the gang started chanting, "Devil dick! Devil dick! Devil dick!" When the painters had finished, they threw the can and brushes in the creek, and the whole group disappeared up the path to the location of the cars.

They were gone, but before they left they rolled him in the dry, loose dirt so that he now had a red crust covering most of his body. He was in pain from the beating and stiff from the dirt crust. It was now quiet under the trestle, and the fire was burning low to a bed of glowing coals. He knew he had to try to get back to Deep Elm and get cleaned up. He gathered his clothes and jacket from the bushes, got dressed, and went up the trail to the railroad tracks. It felt good to get the clothes on because it was getting a lot colder. He knew the tracks led back into Dallas, and he didn't want to be seen on the streets, so he decided to walk the tracks back to the city. It was not only cold, but it was starting to rain. He climbed through the window of a railroad shack that he found along the way. The shack was warmer and out of the rain. In the shack he found a can of coal oil (kerosene) that he used to clean most of the paint off his body. The kerosene fumes burned his nostrils, and the liquid burned his skin. He removed most of the crusty paint from his body, but very little out of his hair. He still looked partly like a recently scrubbed tar baby and partly like a Raggedy Ann Doll with red hair. He smelled like a kerosene stove, and he still looked like he had been tarred and feathered. He still had a strong odor and disheveled appearance, but, at least, he could walk through the city without drawing too much attention to himself. He made it back to Deep Elm and crawled under the building. When it got light in a couple of hours, he was going to get cleaned up and contact his mother who lived on Akard Street in Dallas.

Anne (pronounced Annie) Hadley had come to Dallas shortly after the turn of the twentieth century from Kentucky, and through Jefferson, Texas. She and her husband divorced soon after they arrived, but Anne apparently was well off financially after the divorce. Over the years, she had only one child who she named Orvalee James Clemmons. Anne did not know who the father was because of the nature of her profession. She made up the name so the child's name would not be associated with her name. Orvalee was now known as Radio by most people in Dallas. Sometime after the divorce, Anne became one of the most famous madams and prostitutes in Dallas history.

Anne began her career in "Frogtown" which was a red-light district in Dallas. The area was known as "Frogtown" because when a gentleman visited there, he could hear the croaking frogs in the Trinity river bottoms and in Dallas Branch that led to the river. Once the area became a designated red-light district, it also was referred to as the "reservation." Apparently, Anne made a great deal of money because she soon owned boarding houses and parlor houses which were a higher class of establishment. Most of the prostitutes worked out of "cribs" consisting of two small rooms, one opening to the sidewalk or boardwalk where the women would advertise themselves from the window or door. Several wealthy Dallas businessmen financed establishments in the "reservation" until local sentiment led the city to dissolve the ordinance that established "Frogtown."

Most of the houses of prostitution moved out of the red-light district and eventually were established in various parts of the city. Anne moved her establishment to the Akard Hotel. She lived on the second floor of the building. The building was abandoned except for Anne's place. The lower floors were boarded up, and the windows in the upper floors were broken out. The only other creatures living in the building were bats, rats, and stray cats. The bats flew out of the upper windows in the evening to feast on the millions of mosquitoes that rose from the Trinity river bottoms and invaded the city. The stray cats and rats came and went as they pleased.

Anne was old and looked beyond her years, and she was dying of syphilis. Her hair was falling out, and she had lost her teeth. When Radio would climb the stairs to the second floor, she no longer would open the door. She didn't want him to see the way she looked. She was the only person in the world he knew that he was related to. He adored her in earlier years and still did, but he hadn't seen her in almost a year. She simply slid money and cigarettes under the door to him when he visited her.

After she moved to the hotel, she entertained young men for several years, but now she was too old for the trade. Unfortunately, her reputation was widespread and enduring. She had even changed her name to Ann Hart, but the young men continued to climb the stairs and pound on the door looking for Akard Annie. In recent years, she was harassed so much that she would crack the door to the limit of the security chain and point her 45 automatic pistol through the opening and yell at the boys to "Get the hell out of here." They always stumbled and fell down the stairs to the street, quite frightened at the sight of the pistol. But, the young men continued to come based on her reputation and legacy from years in the past.

Radio knew his mother was a whore, but he deeply loved her, almost worshipped her, and depended on her for financial support. The emotional scars of her profession haunted him for years and continued to affect his life. He loved her and manically hated the men he thought had hurt her in the past. When he was a small child, she would sometimes hide him when she had a customer. Most of the time she hid him in the privy behind the boarding house. But, sometimes it was too cold for that so she hid him in a large chifforobe or clothes wardrobe in her room.

He hated the screams he heard many times as he curled-up in the hiding place. He wanted to come out, but she had sternly ordered him to never come out when she was with a man. He thought she was being hurt and, on most occasions, she was. He dreaded the hiding place and he was tortured the rest of his life by the memories of the violent and never ending shrieking and cursing. As he got older, he avoided the nightmare by living in the streets and only coming around in the daytime. He avoided business hours which were usually from eight o'clock in the evening until midnight or later if customers paid to stay later.

When Radio was six years old, he witnessed one of the most brutal, macabre, barbaric, and gruesome events in the history of Dallas. The event occurred downtown where he spent most of his time as a street urchin and ragamuffin. He had a free run of all of the back alleys, hideouts, and obscure areas of the city. For a six year old, who enjoyed few privileges and advantages, he was clever, resourceful, and wary.

He regularly made the rounds of hotels, bars, and restaurants to scavenge or beg a scrap of food. He went to the back door of the establishment in the alley or at the rear of the building. His primary stops were at the Imperial Bar in the Oriental Hotel, the Old Rathskeller, and the Araby Bar and Restaurant. There were other children who lived in the streets, so he had to move quickly to get the best handouts. He stayed in the shadows and tried to move around Dallas without being noticed.

He was making his rounds one day when he noticed and heard a large crowd of people, all white men, headed for the red stone courthouse, a few blocks away. He didn't like crowds, but he was intensely curious about what such a large gathering could be doing. He immediately headed for the courthouse, taking a different route than the crowd was taking. He got to the courthouse and found a good place to hide to see what was going to happen when the crowd reached the courthouse.

The courthouse was guarded by a line of fifty armed sheriff's deputies and twenty city police officers. Radio didn't move when he saw the crowd of men break through the line and enter the big red stone building. Most of the crowd stayed outside and continued shouting in unison, and sometimes a dozen at a time:

"Kill the nigger, burn the nigger, and hang the nigger."

He couldn't hear the specifics of much of anything, because there was so much screaming and yelling by all of the participants. The men were very angry and agitated, and Radio had never seen so much anger, so he shrunk further back in the shadows. He went into a trance, and then his whole body jerked when he saw a negro man thrown head first from the second story window. He had a rope around his neck. He had heard stories on Deep Elm about lynching out in the county, but he was shocked that he might be seeing a lynching in downtown Dallas.

Radio couldn't tell if the man hit the ground. Quickly the crowd turned and started dragging the man's limp body down the street. Radio could see the crowd had kicked and crushed the man's face until he was covered in blood.

Some in the mob wanted to burn the man, but others wanted to hang him. It looked to Radio that the crowd was headed down the street, and then he lost sight of the mass of people. He darted through the alleys and ran one street over and parallel to the street taken by the crowd. The crowd swelled to over two thousand people who were trotting down the street with the man's body at the end of the rope. Along the way, Radio caught a glimpse of the body, and he could see the man's coat, shoes, and pants were torn off by being dragged on the rough brick street.

Radio would dash ahead of the crowd, hide, and wait for the mass of shouting men, with a few women, to pass. The crowd stopped at the Elks Arch at the corner of Main and Akard streets. The few remnants of clothing that were left on the man were snatched by souvenir hunters. Radio hid in the shadows behind the arch where he could see what was going to happen next. He could see across the street the patrons of the Palace Drugstore crowded into the open second floor windows to watch the crowd below. They had a box seat view of the event.

A man scaled the arch and threw a rope over an arm on a telephone pole next to the arch. Then the mutilated corpse of an elderly, naked, black man was raised to a level where he could be seen by the entire crowd. The crowd burst into a louder level of cheers. Radio was frozen in place. He couldn't feel any sensation in the rest of his body as he watched the lynching. He wanted also to run away in fear, but he was mesmerized by the scene. Before he did run away as fast as his skinny legs would take him, he saw the mob lower the man and cut the rope into pieces as souvenirs. His face went into a trance-like stare and then he giggled.

Radio returned to his mother, and she told him to keep his mouth shut. When he went to Deep Elm, nobody was saying anything about the incident, even though both Dallas newspapers ran stories about the lynching. After the incident, Radio could still feel a collective uneasiness among the white residents of Deep Elm and panic among the black residents. Radio overheard some of the black residents of Deep Elm, after the lynching, discussing plans to leave Dallas and flee to one of the small communities outside of town. They were worried that the lynch mob would strike again and kill many black people like had been done in Texas cities and southern cities in the past. They were fearful of a white lynch mob hanging several black men on the pretense that black citizens were threatening to start a "race riot."

Radio thought about what he had seen, and the thoughts and visions stayed with him for many years. He learned that the racial hatred that he had seen, in his few years of awareness, was much deeper and stronger than he had realized. He now knew the violence he had seen on Deep Elm could erupt among the rich, white, and prominent downtown Dallas residents. He saw that peaceful white men could quickly turn violent. He knew he didn't want to die by being hung. Finally, over time he discovered that not only were none of the participants charged and punished for the crime, but also people in downtown Dallas never expected for anybody to be held accountable for the lynching of the elderly black man.

When Radio was nineteen, he watched a Klan rally of eight hundred hooded individuals in Dallas. Two years later, he and Jimma hid in the shadows and watched another rally by the Klan at Fair Park. Later that year, Klan members took a black man from a hotel and drove him out to a spot on Hutchins Road. They flogged him and used acid to paint "KKK" on his forehead. The event was the "word" on the street in Deep Elm and in the Dallas newspapers, because the crowd took a blindfolded reporter with them to record the event.

As Anne earned more money, she gradually became the "madam" of several boarding houses and managed several "spoiled doves." On many occasions she had to remove a customer who was too drunk or violent to stay in the house. She knew the sheriff and town marshal very well. And, over the years, she knew the local police very well because of her profession. Some of them visited her quite often, so she had widespread influence and quite a lot of money. But now, most of the money was gone. She was forgotten, isolated, and sick.

After the rain stopped, Radio crawled from under the building and tried to stand up. He managed to achieve a hunched-over position. He was cold, hungry, in pain, and stiff. His first thought was to get a cigarette and snag a half-pint of whiskey. He shuffled down the muddy path of Deep Elm toward the brick surface of Elm Street. He still had traces of red paint all over him, especially in his hair. He passed the quiet pool halls, the Phoenix Saloon, the Q. T. Saloon, the Green Parrot Dance Hall, and the Gypsy Tea Room. The usual drunks were passed out in the alleys between the buildings of Deep Elm. The area was usually quiet in the mornings, so he wasn't noticed as he passed the last building, the Dizzy Rabbit Bar.

When he got to the brick paved street, he saw an amazing sight. Groups of young men and men alone were all heading down the street in the same direction. They were coming from all over the city and heading in the same direction. He watched the men go by. He looked up the street and down the street for several minutes. He was mesmerized by the size of the exodus and the determination of so many men. He was scared, curious, and transfixed on the scene. Finally, he got the courage to ask a passing group of men who looked to be nineteen or twenty years old.

"Where y'all going?"

"Over to Commerce Street to enlist in the Army," one of them replied.

"Didn't you hear? The Japanese bombed Pearl Harbor yesterday and the president declared war," another said.

"They might even take a bum like you," a third man said.

The group broke into laughter and continued on their march to enlist. Radio was frozen in one of those go-or-stay moments. He was cold, hungry, tired, and living in the street. He wanted out of his misery. But, the news of war was confusing as he watched more men go by. Leaving the only place he had ever known, and his mother, were frightening thoughts.

Finally, he went with the crowds of young men to sign up for military service. When he got to the recruiting office, the lines were long, but he waited patiently to meet with a recruiter and complete the initial paperwork. After he completed the paperwork, they told him to come back in three days to start his induction tests and physical exams. When he returned, the recruiter told him he had been rejected. He had been classified as 4-F, meaning he was physically, mentally, or morally unfit for service.

*You're an evil bastard, wicked and cursed. Your brain is rotting. You are going to hell. Do you hear me? I said you are wicked. Satan's tool.*

Radio had two serious obsessions. Both of which have caused him to be rejected for military service. He had a history of serious psychiatric and legal problems as a result of one obsession. The Dallas police kept a wary eye on Radio. He was obsessed with girls, twelve to thirteen years old. He may have had deviant desires for these girls, but there wasn't any evidence in his behavior. Nevertheless, he was drawn to them so much that he subjected himself to a great deal of pain and suffering, a pain and suffering that lead him into legal trouble. He surely frightened several children and their parents in downtown Dallas.

When he was in his late teens and early twenties, he would stand in the dark shadows near the entrance to the Majestic Palace Tower, or Rial to theaters and watch people coming to and leaving the movies. He wanted to see the girls. He watched them, all dressed up, as they got out of the fancy cars in front of the theatres. He was mesmerized by the scene, and the girls were the lead actors. They were part of a world in which he had never lived, and it seemed to him that he never would. The scene made him anxious, agitated, scared, and sometimes aroused. His heart would beat faster, and he would feel flushed all over his body. With one exception, he never showed himself or said anything to the people he was watching. When he was younger, he occasionally masturbated when he was sure he couldn't be seen. He also had frequent erotic dreams and fantasies about young girls.

On one occasion, he managed to start a conversation with one of the girls who wasn't with her parents for a brief moment. She was curious about the odd looking young man, and he took advantage of her curiosity by leading her away from the theater. He offered to show her his secret "hideout" down in the Trinity River bottoms, below the bluffs of the city. The two walked south, left the brick pavement, and strolled down a narrow path into the underbrush, high grass, and briar vines. They arrived at the "hideout" which consisted of packing crates, tarpaper, scrap lumber, scrap tin, and old tarps. Radio called the place Sanger House because he had tacked up flattened boxes on the inside walls from Sanger Brothers, Volk Brothers, and Neiman Marcus department stores in Dallas. The décor made him feel a little bit like the wealthy people in town.

The place was well concealed, and the girl was the only other person to have seen the place beside Radio. He had retreated to the place for years for privacy and seclusion. He also used the place as an escape from the Dallas Police when the city made periodic moves to control vagrants and derelicts on the street by arresting them and throwing them in jail.

Sanger House had other serious problems as a place to live. Most of the year, it was consumed with clouds of mosquitoes. Situated in the Trinity River flood plain, standing water from frequent river flooding left the city and Sanger House at the mercy of the biting pests and the malaria they carried. Until the runoff water from upstream was impounded, the three forks of the river ran wild, creating massive floods downstream. As a result, Dallas had experienced several malaria outbreaks since the 1900s. In the city, which sat above the floodplain, the mosquitoes were serious health threat, but in the floodplain, they were intolerable. As a result of the insect situation, Radio could only visit Sanger House when the weather was cold enough to kill the pests or when he was desperate.

The "hideout" was fairly well insulated from the elements, but not secure from wandering critters. Sanger House would periodically be invaded by large, aggressive Texas Diamondback Water Snakes, poisonous water moccasins, opossums, or raccoons. So, Radio would have to be very cautious when he entered the place, especially at night.

When he and the little girl approached Sanger House, Radio started a one way conversation with her by bragging about the place. He told her that many girls like her had visited him. He boasted that famous outlaws lived there years ago, and "river ghosts" sometimes visited. His attempts to impress her resulted in a rambling and wildly exaggerated fantasy, none of which was true. He had never spoken to a girl her age, and nobody had visited the place. The girl giggled, laughed, and sat in a trance for about thirty minutes while he told her tales about the place. Suddenly she changed to being frightened as she glanced up the trail they had come down. She had been gone too long, and she was starting to panic. She cried and screamed. Radio quickly sensed the change and led her back up the path. He knew he was in trouble and had to get her back to the theatre.

*You miserable bastard. You tried to rape and kill her. You're going to die for this. The police are going to shoot you down in the street like a mad dog because you are evil and wicked.*

The little girl ran faster up the trail and continued to scream as she got several yards ahead of him. Radio desperately protested:

"Ma! Ma! I didn't touch her.

I swear, I didn't do anything…………..

Oh, Ma what am I going to do?"

He followed the little girl back to within a block of the theatre and let her go the rest of the way on her own. By this time the city was swarming with cops as they frantically searched for the missing child. Within a few minutes back on the street, the police had Radio in custody and on the way to the Dallas jail. The police threw him in jail and questioned him the next day. He admitted to luring the girl away from the theatre, but insisted he did not harm her. The police knew him well from past minor offenses. In his jail cell, Radio started hearing people whispering about him day and night. This time he was in big trouble, and the result was that he was anxious and frightened about what they were going to do to him.

Within a day, Anne got a personal visit from the chief of police. He gave her the bad news. He said there would be a hearing on Radio's case within a week.

Anne didn't want him to stay in jail, so she called the presiding judge. She knew the judge well. She asked him what he could do to get Radio out of jail and possible prison time. The judge indicated that he was under a lot of public pressure to get Orvalee off the street. He suggested she contact the district attorney.

She knew him well also. Evidently, the girl had told the authorities she hadn't been harmed, so between the district attorney and judge, she got the judge to agree to send Orvalee to Terrell State Hospital, formally known as North Texas Lunatic Asylum. He was to be transferred there and spend six months. All it took was one family member's signature. Anne signed the papers in desperation to keep Orvalee out of prison for kidnapping the little girl. Of course, Orvalee had no knowledge of the proceedings or decisions.

On his twenty fourth birthday, Radio was released from the Dallas Jail into the custody of two large men in white uniforms who had come to the jail to transport him to the state hospital. The two men put Radio in a straight jacket, walked him down the Dallas streets to Union Terminal, and boarded an interurban train bound for Terrell, Texas. Radio enjoyed the train ride because he had only ridden a real train once before. He had always ridden on freight cars on short trips around the city of Dallas. He was apprehensive about where he was going, and the two men on the trip said very little to him on the trip, except that he was going to the hospital. He was checked into the hospital and placed in a stark room. The next day he met several doctors and was given a series of tests. Later the doctors said he was schizophrenic, and he would be receiving treatment for his illness. Radio guessed his diagnosis was because of the little girl who screamed at him sometimes. He also told the doctors about the other voices and people who talked and whispered about him. The doctors seemed confident they could help him, which surprised him because he thought the symptoms would occur the rest of his life. He angrily wondered why no one had ever told him he didn't have to be cursed by the chatter and thoughts in his head.

His first treatment was scheduled for a Monday morning, a week after he had arrived. Radio's overall impression of the hospital was that it was a wonderful place. He slept in a bed. He ate three meals a day. He bathed and shaved regularly. Nurses and orderlies were kind and friendly. His clothes were clean. It was warm in the winter, and the hospital had fans in the summer. And, perhaps best of all, there were no mosquitoes, ticks, rats, body lice, or street thugs.

The part of his stay that he didn't like, after a while, was his lack of freedom to go and come when and where he pleased. His world of the Dallas streets was open and free, and the hospital restricted his movement. He had always been an "outside" person and now he was and "inside" person. In addition, Radio had spent most of his life in social isolation. His interaction with people was very limited, so the confinement kept him psychologically uncomfortable much of the time. He felt trapped with too many people around, to the point that he became panicky from time to time. He thought a lot about trying to run away from the place. But, the hospital was physically comfortable compared to sleeping in alleys and abandoned buildings.

The orderlies came to his room and escorted him to the treatment room. The doctors explained how the procedure worked. He was going to receive electroconvulsive shock therapy, or ECT. They said it would only take a few minutes, and he would feel better after it was over. They strapped a device to his head, held him down, and applied the electrical charge. He convulsed violently and then became limp. They moved him to his room where he rested for a day and a half. He had a severe headache and couldn't remember anything about who or where he was. After several days, he noticed the voices and whisperings were gone. What surprised him was how similar the experience was to the many epileptic seizures he had experienced since he was a child. All of the chattering in his head went away for a while after those seizures. But, they always came back. Anne, his mother, knew he had seizures, but, he guessed, nobody else knew. He didn't grow up or live in a family situation, so no one saw him have a seizure. He always had a warning a seizure was about to occur, and he could hide without others seeing him.

When he was younger, he found two cork bottles in an outhouse behind one of the mansions in north Dallas. One was embossed with Keely's Gold Cure for Drunkenness and the other was embossed with Elepizone, A Certain Cure for Epilepsy. He didn't need the first cure. But, he drank some of the contents of the epilepsy cure. It tasted like a concoction of bitter mud, rotgut whiskey, and fermented fruit. Someone in the big house suffered, like he did, from epilepsy. The sufferer had hidden the bottle in the outhouse, because the affliction was a universal social embarrassment, a sign of sinful behavior, or evidence of evil possession. Radio returned weeks later and drank most of the rest of the cure. Like the resident of the big house, he eventually discovered that it didn't cure epilepsy, and his seizures continued.

One of the hospital volunteers explained to Orvalee that his epilepsy was caused by his parents having prohibited and sinful sex. It was God's punishment for them having sex either after defecation, after bloodletting, in a standing position, on the floor, in a room with the lights on, or in a room with a coffee grinder. The volunteer also explained that his schizophrenia was caused by onanism or masturbation, which was considered self pollution and evil. Orvalee had observed many of the patients on the wards of the hospital openly masturbating, so he assumed that what the volunteer had said, must have been true. It also verified what the little girl had said to him many times. Late that night in the hospital, she visited him again.

*See, I told you. You are wicked, an evil person. God is punishing your mother and he is punishing you for her sins and yours. You're both going to burn in the flames of hell forever. Now the doctors and everyone else in the hospital knows about the terrible sins that have been committed. Ha! Ha! Ha!*

His ECT sessions were scheduled for Monday mornings for the duration of his hospitalization. The rest of his schedule consisted of outdoor activities, church services on Sunday mornings and Wednesday evenings, and occasional special programs from volunteers in the community. After he had been in the hospital two weeks, a nurse named Miss Putorff started coming around and visiting him quite regularly. She was older than Radio. She had high cheekbones, and her hair was pulled up and secured tightly on her head. Radio thought she looked nice and noticed she acted friendly to him. He found out she was known a "Putter" by other residents of the hospital. On a Friday, the nurse approached him and said she needed help moving some furniture and mattresses from a storage room. He followed her into the storage room. She took out her keys and locked the door behind them. She immediately faced him, pulled down his pants, squatted down, and administered her version of shock treatment. He was overwhelmed, unprepared, and confused. His body became rigid, and his eyes rolled back in his head. When she thought he was sufficiently prepped for the primary therapy, she took him to one of the mattresses and gave him the full therapeutic intervention. After they finished, she unlocked the door, left it unlocked, and went back to her duties in the hospital. To him, the furniture in the storeroom intensely smelled like mustard. He helped her "move furniture," every Friday, for two months. After the first session in the storeroom, Radio was overcome by the new experience. Later he became completely infatuated with the nurse. He thought she was the most beautiful woman he had ever seen, and he looked for her return on Fridays. She was all he could think about during the week, and as Friday approached, he got very excited, emotionally apprehensive, and sexually aroused. On one Friday, she didn't come and take him to the storage room. She never returned, and the rumor in the hospital was that she had been transferred to the state hospital in Austin. When she stopped meeting him, he became very blue, sullen, and grouchy. While he was seeing her, he lost track of the surroundings in the hospital. His preoccupation with her voice, hair, perfume, beauty, and body caused him to lose some psychological awareness of anything in the periphery outside his surroundings. He spent the week waiting for her. Now he had nothing to wait for. Now he noticed how stark, ugly, and sterile his surroundings were. The only beauty in his life disappeared.

His fantasies and dreams about young girls disappeared while he was in the hospital. It wasn't clear whether the decline was due to the ECT or Miss Putter's intervention. Over the years, he forgot most of what happened in the hospital, but he never forgot her. After six months, he was put on an interurban train in Terrell and returned to Dallas. Radio walked back to Deep Elm and continued with his life before the incident with the little girl. Few people noticed derelicts and vagrants, so he was largely unnoticed as he lived in the shadows of the Dallas shantytown. Years later he summoned the courage to return to Sanger House. When he got to a point on the bluff where he could see the river bottom, he was stunned to see that Sanger House was gone and the Dallas artesian city spring had been razed. Both were in the process of being covered by a concrete football stadium. He had seen Sanger House flooded before, but now it was gone. He turned, left the site, and never returned.

The other uncontrolled obsession that Radio had was with shiny, polished, fancy, black automobiles. He knew how to drive, but had never owned or driven a coup or sedan. When he was younger, he had worked as a helper on an ice delivery truck. The driver let him occasionally drive the truck. Living on the street in Deep Elm, he had learned how to "hot wire" a car in order to steal it, but he had never stolen a car.

He had an intense desire to drive one of the shiny black cars, but like other things in his life, the cars were far out of reach for a poor person. There were many fancy cars in Dallas, so he was surrounded by the object of his obsession. One morning in his wanderings, he crossed the viaduct over the Trinity River connecting Dallas to Oak Cliff. The time was less than ten years before the bombing of Pearl Harbor when he was in his early twenties. He liked to go to the auto repair yard and shop located at the southern end of the viaduct in Oak Cliff. It was one of his favorite places to spend time. The owner would let him squat in the repair shops and the yard where the cars would be parked. He liked the smell of the oil and grease and the sight of disabled cars, scattered around the repair yard. He could squat among the tires, radiators, and car body parts and not be noticed by the customers coming and going. He liked the repair shop, and he liked to hold a stick and use it to fiddle with the discarded nuts, bolts, gaskets and springs lying on the ground. The owner seemed to tolerate him as long as he stayed out of the way and blended in with the junk cars and discarded parts. He also tolerated Radio's giggling when Radio hid behind the cars.

One day, like other days, he visited with the mechanics and watched the people come and go at the repair shop. On this particular day, he observed a young man drive up in a black Ford V8 sedan. The young man was well dressed and he seemed to know the owner of the shop quite well. Radio was impressed by sight of a man so young having such a new and expensive car.

The young man left in another car that had accompanied him to the shop. Radio was immediately fixated on the Ford. He went over and squatted down next to it, so close he almost touched it.

"Don't be touching that Ford, boy," the owner directed.

"That's Clyde's car," he added.

"Clyde don't want nobody messin' with his cars," he said in a serious voice.

Radio didn't know who Clyde was, but he seemed to be a man who must be rich or famous. He continued to be amazed and bewildered that someone so young could own such a fancy and expensive car. Later in the afternoon, the owner of the car returned to the repair shop to get the car. Radio was still there admiring the Ford.

"You like that car kid?" Clyde asked.

"I shore do," replied Radio.

"That there's a really fast car...........You ever ride in one?" Clyde asked.

"No sir. I've never been in one," Radio admitted.

"How would you like to ride with me and my friends up to Oklahoma and Missouri?" Clyde asked.

"Ye-haw. That would be something. I wanna go," Radio exclaimed.

"Tell you what. You be here at nine in the morning and you can go with us," Clyde promised.

"I'll be here for sure. I'm ready to go," Radio said.

Clyde drove the Ford away, and Radio took off on a run back across the river to Deep Elm. The next morning he met the group at the repair shop. He was truly ready because he didn't have anything to do, anybody to tell about the trip, or any arrangements to be made. He met the group which consisted of Clyde, his girlfriend, and another man. Radio rode in the back seat with the other man, and the group headed through Dallas, up East Grand Avenue. Nobody in the car had much to say which was fine with Radio because he wasn't much for conversation himself.

Radio immediately noticed all of the handguns and rifles in the car. He hadn't seen many guns on Deep Elm. He had seen an occasional derringer or pocket gun, but these guns looked very big. He knew this group wasn't cops, so he suspected they were outlaws. The guns and the quiet group made his fear and anxiety rise, and so he started bragging about himself. He bragged that he had been to Oklahoma and Missouri many times. Living alone most of his life, Radio did not develop sophisticated and age appropriate social conversation skills. So, he bragged a lot which quickly became annoying to others. The black Ford, with its strange collection of characters, continued up East Grand Avenue and stopped at the Pig Stand Barbecue. A carhop came to the driver's window and Clyde ordered sandwiches.

Radio didn't have any money, even fifty cents, for a sandwich. Clyde ordered Radio a sandwich and a Coke. After the meal the group went a short distance to where the road name changed to Garland Road and then to the White Rock Lake spillway to see if they could cool off in the water cascading over the natural rock formations. It was a good place to swim if there was enough water coming over the dam. They pulled the cars into the parking area and soon saw that there wasn't enough water to be able to splash around and cool off. The group then reversed their course and headed to the northwest, up Gaston Avenue to Abrams Road to the Richardson Pike toward Oklahoma.

As soon as Radio finished his meal and after seeing White Rock Lake, he began talking about the legend of "The lady of White Rock Lake," a local ghost who is said to appear around a certain part of the park surrounding the lake. When the group was at the spillway, they were near the spot. The legend had been told around the Dallas area at least as early as the 1930s. The legend was particularly popular on Deep Elm where it was embellished, changed, and circulated for years. It was known all over the city, but the residents of Deep Elm seemed to relish legends about wealthier north Dallas citizens. They were also quite suggestible and superstitious when ghosts were included in the story, so rumors and gossip flourished in the small community.

The legend was about a young lady who allegedly drowned in White Rock Lake. Her ghost had been seen by several couples visiting the park at night. In most of the sightings, a couple was parked at one of the many available spaces around the lake. They had steered a car off the road and parked facing the water on East Lawther Drive. The road around the lake had been a popular parking area for young couples for years for people who now had access to automobiles. According to the legend, on a hot summer night a young couple parked at one of the spaces facing the lake. When they turned on the headlights of the car to leave the spot, a white figure approached the car. They soon recognized that it was a young girl dressed in a long sheer white dress that was dripping wet. She seemed confused and spoke to them with hesitation as if in a trance. She said she needed to get home immediately. She stated she had been on a sailboat that had overturned. The other people on the boat were safe, and she needed to get home. The couple didn't recognize her as a ghost or apparition. She seemed to be very real to them. The girl got into the car and gave the couple an address on the south side of Dallas. The couple was anxious about the young lady and as they got closer to the address, to make sure of the location, they turned to the rear seat to ask directions. The seat was empty but still wet. The couple was very surprised at her disappearance, but continued to the address she had given. They went to the address and were met at the door by a man who appeared to be worried.

The couple told him the story of the girl at the lake.

The man was very disturbed by the story and indicated that several couples had come to the house with the same story. He told them that three weeks ago his daughter was drowned while sailing on White Rock Lake.

Radio had heard various versions of the story over the years while living on Deep Elm. But now, he used the story to impress his fellow travelers. He told them he knew the lady very well. In fact, they were lovers. He said he talked to her all the time. He bragged and embellished the story to the point that Clyde told him to "Shut up the crazy talk." By the time Radio had sufficiently annoyed and scared the group, they had arrived at a swimming hole not far from the road in the small community of Vickery. Clyde planned to stop at the place on the way to Oklahoma. The place where they stopped was a well known spring-fed pool at the bottom of the intersection of several deep ravines. People came from around the area to swim in the cool spring water. Many years later, the pool was developed and constructed into a formal swimming pool and park known as Vickery Park.

The trip with Radio to the swimming hole had gotten on the nerves of the group, so when Radio went into the bushes up one of the ravines to pee, the other three dashed to the car and drove off. When Radio returned to the pool the group was gone, so he had to find a way back to Dallas. He begged other people at the pool for a few coins and rode the interurban electric train back to Dallas. The interurban ran parallel to the Richardson Pike out to Plano and back to Dallas. Radio never made it to Oklahoma or Missouri, but he did get to ride in the shiny black sedan.

Radio continued to go to the Dallas recruiting office to enlist in the Army. He tried several times and finally in May, 1942 he was accepted and classified as I-A, and suitable for military service. It's not clear why the Army relaxed the requirements for enlistment that allowed Radio to be accepted, but the military was planning for an invasion of Europe and may have been anticipating the need for many replacement troops.

More than likely, he was reclassified because the draft boards around the country were not meeting their quotas for draftees. At first, married men were not drafted, and later fathers were not drafted until 1943. This regulation led to a significant and inevitable "marriage boom." Radio got caught in a political pressure to draft men who were not working, homeless, or found in pool rooms and saloons. He was previously found to be "emotionally unstable," but high level officials in the War Department blamed the classification on "momism," which resulted from women who had failed the elementary motherly function of weaning their children emotionally as well as physically.

Whatever the reason, Radio was instructed to report to Camp Swift,

Texas within two weeks. Radio had spent most of his life in social isolation and withdrawal, and now he was going to be thrust into a close, complex, and intense social environment.

Radio dreaded telling Anne he had enlisted in the Army. He was scared that he would die in a muddy ditch on Deep Elm or be beat to death by one of the gangs. He was also scared of leaving his only friend and relative. He dreaded leaving her alone and being alone himself. Now he was trapped and would have to tell her. He knew nothing about Army life, but he knew most of the men in Dallas his age and younger had gone off to the war. Deep Elm had become a very quiet place. Many of the people were gone, and many of the businesses were closed, boarded up, or vacant. The previously bustling shanty town was almost deserted.

The little girl hadn't screamed at him in a long time. He thought the state hospital may have cured him of her violent visits. He knew he would have to make the walk  to the Akard Hotel and tell his mother he was leaving. Before he did, he spent a day and night at Sanger House in the river bottom to think about what he was about to do.

That night a flock of Whistling Ducks sang him to sleep. They were on their way back north, and they had landed on a small pond where Turtle Creek ran toward the river. It was a peaceful place, and that night there were no mosquitoes.

He eventually walked to where the old hotel was on Akard Street. The sun had gone down, and it was dark when he arrived. He stopped at the bottom of the stairs that led from the street to the second floor. He lit up a cigarette. He took a couple of puffs and started up the stairs. The stairway was dark, and the walls were covered with years of accumulated graffiti, smoke residue, and dirt dauber nests. The floor and stairs were also covered in a dark brown splatter stain left by years of chewing tobacco, mixed with spittle, which had been ejected and deposited by visitors to the building in the absence of a convenient spittoon.

The wooden stairs groaned and creaked with each step he took toward the second floor. Anne lived at the door to the left at the top where there was a small landing. Radio hadn't seen his mother in many months, and he did what he always did when he visited her. He sat quietly on the landing and smoked a cigarette. She knew it was him from the sound of the steps on the stairs and the cigarette smoke drifting under the bottom of the door. He heard her dragging her chair over the wooden floor to a place on the opposite side of the door where he was sitting. The two people sat opposite each other with the door between them for some time, and then he began pushing individual cigarettes under the door to her. He knew she didn't go out of the apartment anymore, so she always needed some "smokes."

After a while he mustered the courage to say:

"Ma,...........I joined the Army."

She didn't say anything. The two sat in silence for several minutes. Then he could hear her crying. He hadn't heard her cry since he was a child and Anne worked as a whore in Frogtown. He heard her cry a lot in those days. She pushed fifty dollars under the door, and then drug her chair back across the room to the window where she spent most of her days and would spend the rest of her life looking out of the window at Akard Street. She was too frail and near death to do anything else.

Radio descended the stairs to the street and in June of 1942, Orvalee James Clemmons boarded a train at Union Station in Dallas bound for Camp Swift near Bastrop, Texas. He never returned to Bob-O-Links.

# CHAPTER 3

## ZEPHYR

First Lieutenant Art Shafer and his family headed west on Highway 80 bound for Camp Swift, Texas. The trip on the first day had been slow and tiring. The highway was congested by Army vehicle convoys. Long lines of equipment, jeeps, trucks, ambulances, artillery pieces, battle tanks on trailers, and open trucks full of soldiers moved slowly across the country in both directions. At one time, all they could see in front of them was an enormous, olive drab colored, steel monster being transported on a trailer designed to carry Army tanks.

They were caught behind an Army tank being moved to one of the military bases in the west, so for miles they looked at the metal tracks, a white star painted on the armor plated rear deck, and the mud covered underbelly of the huge machine. Caught behind the convoy, it was difficult to pass the long line of vehicles in front of them on the two lane highway. In addition, the pace of the convoy was slow and deliberate. The family began to realize that the trip was going to take longer than they anticipated. Mile after mile they snaked behind vehicle convoys. When there was an opportunity, Art would swing the Dodge into the opposite lane of traffic and scoot ahead to one of the rare openings in the line of vehicles. He was thankful that he had bought the Dodge that had enough power to make the vehicle passes. Still, they could only manage a speed of thirty-five miles an hour.

Highway 80 was busy with military traffic because of mobilization for war, and the highway connected the bases in the east, across the southern row of states, with the bases in the west, including Fort Polk, Fort Sam Houston, Camp Hood, Fort Bliss, Camp Wolters, and Camp Swift. The family spent the night in a hotel in Jackson, Mississippi.

Art would have liked to have gone further, but he feared that they wouldn't be able to find a place to spend the night after they left Jackson, especially in the delta country of the Mississippi River. He also feared that he hadn't lost all of his "yankee" accent after his brief stay in Atlanta and Dallas. Jackson was racially segregated, but the delta was poorly developed and rural. He didn't like the prospect of looking for a hotel in the delta. He felt more comfortable crossing the delta the next morning.

They crossed the Mississippi Delta and headed for Texas. The congestion on the highway got much worse as they neared Fort Polk, Louisiana. They encountered more military traffic going to and coming from the fort.

Art received his transfer orders June 3rd when he finished the Basic Infantry Training School and the Division Officers Course at Fort Benning and a promotion to First Lieutenant. The order specified he was to report "not prior to nor later than June 19, 1942," for duty. All of the one hundred nineteen officers in his class were directed to report to Camp Carson, Colorado or Camp Swift, Texas. They were all First or Second Lieutenants. He was assigned to command a company of inductees at Camp Swift, a training base that had just opened. He had inquired around Fort Benning about what Camp Swift was like. The scuttlebutt was that it was a hot, dry, and primitive "hell hole." The camp was so new that there was very little information among the troops about the camp. One officer told him that most of the town of Bastrop near the camp didn't have public sewers. Based on what people told him, Art and Skip decided to look for a place to stay in Austin, Texas, about twenty miles west of the camp. Austin, they predicted, would have more rental apartments or houses available for the family. The family had only one car, so Skip would need to be close enough to a grocery store to be able to walk to get what the family needed. It didn't seem to Art that the short drive to Camp Swift every morning would be too difficult and time consuming. Officers with families were allowed to live off the base, but officers without families or single officers were allowed to live on the base in the BOQ or bachelor officer's quarters. Some officers chose to leave home and their families behind, so they stayed in the BOQ. Art and Skip decided to stay together during his stateside assignments, and she would follow him from place to place.

Finally, after the family crossed the Louisiana border and entered Texas, Art turned the Dodge to the southwest and headed toward Austin. He was now in familiar territory. In Texas, there were fewer convoys, and the family made better driving time. But a major problem of the trip was getting enough gas to continue the trip without getting stranded on the side of the road. Gas stations were scarce. A station may not have any gas when you found one because the government was rationing gas so there would be enough for military vehicles and the war effort.

Art had plenty of gas coupons. The problem was that the gas tank on the Dodge wasn't large enough to make it from place to place, gas station to gas station, or fill up to fill up. There were few stations along the route, especially in small towns. Cars were a luxury and many people didn't own one. Art decided, after worrying about getting enough gas on the trip, that he would get a second tank installed on the Dodge when he got to Austin. Installing a second tank was illegal, but he was determined to beat the coupon glut and gas shortage problem.

Art rented a small house on the south side of the river in Austin and moved the family into the new residence. After the family moved in, Art drove them to see his brother Ed who was stationed at Camp Barkley in Abilene, Texas. He had over a week before he was supposed to report to Camp Swift. He planned to get to Camp Swift headquarters early on the Monday morning he was supposed to report. Camp Swift was twenty-eight miles east of Austin and seven miles north of the city of Bastrop. He decided to leave an hour early in order to give himself plenty of time. So, he left at seven a.m. and drove east on the two-lane highway to Bastrop. He soon discovered he had made a serious miscalculation. He had only traveled a few miles when the traffic on the highway was either moving very slowly or was completely stopped. The narrow road was backed up with busses, military vehicles, flat-bed trucks loaded with lumber and tarpaper, cars, and delivery trucks. It looked to him that every resource in the region was headed to the new camp. Every intersection was a traffic jam, and vehicles were pulled off the side of the road in both directions.

It became obvious he wasn't going to be able to arrive early at the camp. In fact, it looked more like he was going to be late to report for duty.

"Damn, this is frustrating. What a huge mess," he said.

He could see soldiers hitchhiking on both sides of the road. They were trying to get to Austin or back to the camp. Many soldiers were abandoning busses that were stopped on the road with flat or worn-out tires. Tires were rationed, so the worn tires were very undependable and unreliable. The treadless tires were commonly referred to as "bald eagles."

The Dodge slowly rolled along the road, and he couldn't do anything about the traffic mess. He was trapped. All he could do was curse the chaos. He was sitting in the limbo of a traffic hell when he heard a sound coming at him. In a second, the Dodge shook as a blast of airplane engines passed very low over the car, kicking up dust and blowing the grass and mesquite trees around the road in a whirlwind of debris. The sound was deafening. He looked to the left and saw the tail section and silhouette of a C-47 troop carrier flying low as it disappeared behind the trees.

"What the hell was that?"

Then another blast shook the Dodge. A few minutes later another blasted across the highway. He then realized that he was directly under a flyway for Bergstrom Air Base that was a troop carrier training center. The C-47s never stopped the flyovers. He finally got far enough down the highway so that he wasn't in the flight path anymore. The Dodge was covered with dust, inside and out.

Art finally reached the iron bridge over the Colorado River, crossed the bridge into Bastrop on the east side of the river, went through Bastrop, and headed east of the town. Camp Swift was located about seven miles north of the small town. As he passed through the city, he could see a Missouri-Kansas-Texas train parked in the town with hundreds of inductees exiting the passenger cars. They all wore civilian clothes, of course, and their clothes ranged from the poorest rags to the finest suits. They looked like they came from all walks of life, ranging from farm boys to bankers. Many were carrying small suitcases. Art knew they wouldn't be keeping the suitcases very long. Sergeants were shouting orders, forming the inductees into lines, and loading them into the rear of  two and a half ton trucks, some open and some covered with canvas. The trucks rumbled through Bastrop and headed to the camp. These were the men that Art was going to have to turn into fighting men. They didn't look, to him, to be very promising in their present state of disorder and confusion. For many, this would be the first time they had been out of their hometown. They were only a small sample of the millions of men that were being mobilized and trained for combat.

As the Dodge rolled slowly through the streets of Bastrop, Art realized that he had made the best choice of moving the family to Austin. Bastrop was a very small town with a few streets lined with large old homes surrounded by the largest pecan trees he had ever seen. The city sat near the banks of the Colorado River, and soldiers could be seen all over the small town. The bus station, post office, and Western Union office were busy, around the clock, with soldiers and military vehicles. As he approached State Highway 95, he encountered MPs at every intersection as traffic and congestion increased to and from the camp.

His other impression of the small town was that it appeared to be "dry" with no liquor, beer, or wine sales. He didn't see any liquor stores, bars, or nightclubs in or near the town. This meant that the soldiers must be obtaining passes to go to Austin to drink a beer. He thought: *What a mess............ nothing for the inductees to do.............nothing to drink.............no place to relax and let off steam. They have to go thirty miles to the west to find something to do.* Now he understood the cause for all of the busses on the highway to Austin. He headed north up Highway 95, passing a sign to the state park, and approached the entrance to Camp Swift. As he approached the entrance, to his right, he saw more MPs directing traffic in and out of the camp. To his left, he saw that the MKT railroad tracks ran parallel and next to the highway. For about a half a mile, freight and passenger cars were on the tracks. Men were disembarking from the passenger cars and equipment, freight, and vehicles were being unloaded from box and flatbed cars. On one of the larger crates somebody had written: "KILROY WAS HERE," a popular graffiti marking during war mobilization. The scene was a tangle of confusion and congestion in a cloud of white dust. Trucks crossed the railroad tracks, passed in front of him, and headed for the camp entrance. Above the white dust cloud, he could see a tall white sign alongside the tracks that read: "Camp Swift Station." He passed through the entrance to the camp which consisted of two wooden pine poles with a plywood sign at the top, and headed for the headquarters building. The headquarters building was clearly marked, "Camp Swift 1942."

As he drove the short distance to the headquarters, he could see the layout of the camp. It was vast, bleak, and barren except for a few completed buildings and buildings under construction. All of the trees and brush had been removed, and the grass was mowed close to the ground. All of the buildings were widely separated. He concluded the design of the camp was to reduce fire danger. The roads were made of crushed white rock. A strong southeastern breeze had spawned a large dust devil that picked up bits of grass and spun them skyward in a barely visible column. When the dust devil crossed the white rock roads, it transformed into an easily visible white column of dust that quickly disappeared when it crossed back into the field. The one story headquarters building was covered with white siding. Most of the other barracks were covered in black tar paper. He could see crews digging trenches for water and sewer, crews stringing power lines, Bell Telephone trucks stringing phone lines, and crews unloading trucks with building supplies. It appeared that there were many civilian contractors involved in constructing the camp. In the near distance, he could see crews constructing two elevated water tanks and flatbed trucks hauling brush and trees that had been removed from the firing ranges. He had never seen so much activity in one place, and the speed and enormity of the mobilization was staggering and confusing. Vehicles were traveling in all directions on the geometric maze of streets stretching as far as he could see.

All of the activity kicked up dust from the roads and blew it across the vast plain of the camp. Soldiers in khaki uniforms were walking in all directions, sometimes disappearing in the clouds of blowing dust. Barracks and other buildings were under construction up and down the wide crushed rock streets.

Art parked the Dodge among the many vehicles parked at the headquarters building. He was met by his new orderly, Private Eugene Shearer.

Private Shearer had been waiting for him with the Jeep he would be driving around the camp. The Jeep had a canvass top, and it looked like a new vehicle. Private Shearer waited in the Jeep while Art went into the headquarters. The camp was hiring people, so there was a steady supply as indicated by a line of civilians looking for jobs and being hired. They were going in and out of the headquarters building. Art could see it was a busy place. In addition, other officers, like himself, were arriving daily and quickly reporting to the camp commander, He opened the door and immediately heard the staccato clattering of typewriter keys being whacked against paper as the bells on typewriters rang when carriages were thrown to start the next line of type and round of clatter. The headquarters was filled with civilian typists who were typing the induction records for thousands of incoming soldiers. The typists were all women. They were typing records, inserting carbon paper between the sheets of paper, and throwing wadded balls of paper in all directions when they made a typing error. Most were chewing gum or drinking "Cokes." There didn't seem to be a square foot of space in the headquarters building. Art didn't see how anybody could hear anything over the continuous noise of the typewriters.

In an office to the side, Art reported to and met the commanding officer of the camp, Lieutenant Colonel Shurtz. The meeting was brief because the commander was very busy as personnel went in and out of his office and other officers were reporting daily. Art had been assigned to A Company as the company commander in the 379th Battalion of the newly formed 95th Division. His orders had arrived at Camp Swift, so they knew he was coming. The cadre or original officers for the 95th Division came from the 2nd Infantry Division which was stationed at Fort Sam Houston in San Antonio, Texas.

Art completed the required paperwork and obtained a locator card that he had to turn in to the Postal Officer so that he could receive mail while he was at the camp. He was told that he needed a bumper tag to get into the camp. They issued him one, and it read "0-325, SWIFT." He installed the tag on the front bumper of the Dodge when he got back to Austin. Finally, he asked for a map of the camp. The clerk looked confused by the request, but disappeared into one of the side rooms and returned with a map of the camp. Art unrolled the large map and discovered that it was simply a survey map of the boundaries of the camp. No roads or structures were noted on the survey map.

It was obvious to Art at this time that the camp was too new for such formal documents as a detailed map. He also had a fearful realization that most of the people in the headquarters didn't know where anything was located on the camp property. The next thing he needed to do was to get to the quartermaster to draw his additional khakis and field equipment. One of the clerks knew which building was the one where the quartermaster was located, so Art headed out the door with directions. He told his new orderly to meet him back at A Company barracks in an hour and to direct the company executive officer to have the company assembled for inspection at that time.

He drove the Dodge to the building that housed the quartermaster, went in, and tried to draw his equipment. The quartermaster only gave him some khaki uniforms. Art asked where his field equipment was. The man said they didn't have any yet, and he would have to order some for him. He also said it could take a month or more for it to come to Camp Swift because there were thousands of orders being placed all over the country for field equipment for new officers. This meant Art wouldn't have a helmet, pistol belt, canteen, or first aid kit. Art was beginning to see how unprepared the Army was for training. The quartermaster ordered his field equipment. He asked the clerk about the rumors he had heard at Fort Benning about a new semiautomatic rifle and high-top, buckle combat boots that had been adopted for combat by the Army. The clerk didn't know anything about the items and hadn't seen either one. Art knew rumors were highly unreliable and erroneous, so he dropped the subject. He parked the Dodge next to his new Jeep in front of the barracks for A Company. The building was covered in black tar paper so Art knew it would be hot as an oven inside.

The company of soldiers was assembled in front of the barracks and divided into four platoons of men. Art was irritated as he got out of the Dodge because it was after ten o'clock in the morning and he had planned to review the company at eight in the morning, two hours earlier. The company executive officer, a sergeant, was standing in front of the company with a soldier holding a guidon consisting of a small triangular flag attached to the top with a "A" stenciled on it.

He approached the sergeant and stood face-to-face with him so that the sergeant had his back to the company, and Art was looking over the man's shoulder at the assembled men. Art could immediately tell the trainees were very young. Some looked sixteen years old. He could see that their fatigue uniforms didn't fit very well. Most of the shirts and pants were too big for the younger trainees. He quickly addressed the sergeant.

"Good morning sergeant, I'm your new company commander, Lieutenant Shafer."

"Good morning sir."

"Let's do a roll call sergeant and see who we have here," Art said.

"Yes sir," the sergeant replied.

The sergeant took the clipboard from under his arm and started calling names, starting with the first platoon. As the roll was called, five or six men were absent from first, second, third, and fourth platoons. Art mentally noted that there were over twenty men missing from the company. When the sergeant was finished calling the roll, he turned and faced Art.

"Sergeant, where are the rest of the men in this company?" Art asked.

"They're in the hospital and the stockade sir. Most are in the stockade," the sergeant replied.

"What are the others in the hospital for?" Art asked.

"Chiggers sir," the sergeant loudly proclaimed.

Several of the assembled soldiers snickered loud enough for Art to hear them. Art knew they laughed because it was humorous to soldiers from the southern part of the country that soldiers from the north were so susceptible to a variety of insect bites, particularly chiggers.

"Sergeant, step forward and tell me so that everyone in this camp doesn't hear you," Art ordered sarcastically.

"Yes sir," the sergeant responded sheepishly.

"The men are in for chiggers and uh………..scorpions…………ticks…………poison ivy…………..snake bite………….Private Avery back there in second platoon got bit by a Copperhead last week and was sick and swollen up for several days,………..and, uh heat exhaustion, sir. The scorpions are really bad. They're in the barr……."

Art had heard enough, so he interrupted the sergeant.

"Okay, sergeant I'll take care of getting the men out of the hospital. What about the men in the stockade?" Art asked.

"I don't know sir. They don't tell us much about them," the sergeant replied.

"Okay, how do I get them out?"

"Well, sir the other company commanders have to go to the stockade at six a.m., fill out paperwork, and then check them out to get them released back to the company."

"Six a.m.?" Art confirmed.

"Yes sir," the sergeant replied.

During the conversation, Art had been observing the company and discovered several obvious missing items in the ranks of the men.

"Sergeant, where are the other officers……..uh, I mean the platoon leaders?"

"We don't have any sir……..never have had any. We've all arrived in the last two weeks. Major Hill comes by and gives us our daily assignments," the sergeant replied.

"Okay, well where are their weapons?" Art continued to inquire and remain as calm as possible.

"We don't have any…………we had some of those Navy contract wooden Springfield drill rifles, but they came and took them away. And, we shoot the real Springfields on the range, but they keep them at the range, and we've only been there two times," the sergeant replied.

"Okay sergeant, where are the combat boots for the men?" Art asked after he observed that the men were wearing civilian shoes of all descriptions.

"We don't have any sir," the sergeant replied.

"How did you get promoted to sergeant, Sergeant Wilson?" Art asked.

"One year in a military academy........I guess sir," the sergeant replied.

In order to add a little levity to the formal and stiff situation, Art asked: "Is there somewhere around here to get a cold beer, sergeant?"

The sergeant smiled and replied, "Yes sir, there are some good places in town, about ten minutes away."

Art realized that the small town of Bastrop was "wet," and he just didn't see any liquor stores, bars, or beer joints when he came through the town. The sergeant looked relieved that the company now had a commander and the pressure of command was off of him.

"Where is your hometown, sergeant?" Art asked.

"Atlanta, Georgia, sir," the sergeant replied.

"I've been there and it's a fine place."

"Thank you, sir."

"What about their tests?" Art asked.

"They've all been through the camp hospital and completed their physicals, shots, psych's, and dentals," the sergeant answered.

"Good."

"And they all passed," the sergeant bragged with a large grin on his face.

"I'm sure," Art said, knowing that it was widely understood that in this time of mobilization, it would be rare for an inductee to fail any of the tests given for  acceptance to active duty in the Army. The men in the company, still standing at attention, were getting restless, so he finished the conversation with:

"Okay sergeant, you've been very helpful. I'm going to try to find out a little more about what's going on here. In the meantime, get the men ready for inspection in the morning. I'm going to inspect the barracks at 7 a.m. after I get the other men out of jail."

"Yes sir," the sergeant loudly responded.

Art got in the Dodge and drove away. He was amused by the sergeant's southern drawl, accent, and choice of words and he thought:

*This is a helluva kettle of fish. I'm supposed to get these men ready for combat and they don't even have boots or weapons. Shit, what a SNAFU.*

The sergeant turned to face the men and shouted:

"Alright, you peckerwoods get the barracks shipshape. First platoon, you're in charge of cleaning the latrine and showers; Second platoon, the outside grounds; Third platoon, the floors; and Fourth platoon, you've got trash detail. Get on it and get it done. FALL OUT!"

The next morning, Art had to get up at five a.m. to get to the stockade by seven a.m. to get the men in his company released. The stockade looked like all of the other tar paper covered barracks except for the MP vehicles parked in front, a six-by-six truck and two jeeps with "MILITARY POLICE" stenciled in white letters on both sides. He went into the stockade and completed the paperwork to release the men in the company. The inside of the building was divided into hog wire partitions on each side of a central walkway down the center of the building. The stockade was full of men behind the hog wire.

An MP brought the line of men out and ordered them to stand at attention. Art went down the line of men, stopping at each man and looking each man in the face at close range. He addressed the first soldier:

"What are you in here for soldier?"

"Drunk and disorderly, sir," the rigid soldier replied.

Art went to the next soldier and asked the same question and the man replied:

"I went to Austin without a pass, sir."

"So, you were AWOL?" Art quickly responded.

"Yes sir," the soldier agreed.

Art went down the line of men and confronted each one. It was soon obvious that the camp was very lenient with issuing passes to the soldiers to go to Austin. A bus company had even been contracted to take them there if the soldier paid for the ride to Austin. They could return free in the back of a six-by-six truck. There was an MP station in Austin, so the MPs were very quick and efficient in apprehending and rounding up trouble makers. As a result, many soldiers were in the stockade on week nights and over the weekend, so Art was going to have to get up very early almost every morning to get the missing members of the company back to the barracks for their training.

Three fourths of the way down the line of men, Art got a big surprise. He turned and faced the next man in the line and he was face-to-face with the ball washer, named Radio, who had been at Bob-O-Links golf course in Dallas. He was sure it was him, but shocked that he would be in the Army at Camp Swift. He was now in fatigues. He was clean shaven, and his hair was cut much shorter. He was also standing straighter than he remembered him to be at Bob-O-Links. Except for facial features, he looked like all of the other inductees, but he wasn't. This was Radio.

*How could this be him? How could he be here? Does he know who I am?*

He looked down at the name tag and it read, "Clemmons."

*Keep a poker face and don't let any of the men suspect you might know this man.*

Art quickly asked the man from the past, "Where is your hometown soldier?"

"Dallas, sir."

The soldier didn't blink, and Art waited to move on for what seemed to him to be several minutes, but was only several seconds. Art realized that he now had to ask another soldier where his hometown was so that the group of men wouldn't suspect he knew Private Clemmons. He asked another soldier about his hometown and the soldier replied:

"Colbert County, Alabama, sir."

Art didn't know where this particular hometown was, but he didn't care because he was now out of suspicion of knowing the man from Dallas. He couldn't be sure the ball washer had recognized him, and he didn't know whether he might in the future as he trained the company in preparation for their deployment. Fortunately, the strange man from Dallas would be under the direct command of his platoon leader.

Once he had looked at each of the prisoners face-to-face, he stepped back several steps and said:

"You men double time it back to the barracks and get ready for inspection at 0700. I'm going to inspect the barracks and everything better be in shipshape and policed up. Get all of the beer or whiskey out of those foot-lockers and anything else that shouldn't be in them."

"But sir, the barracks are over a mi..........," one of the men complained.

"Get your butts going right now," Art interrupted sternly.

Art found out quickly that he was going to have to spend a lot of time at the stockade, perhaps several mornings a week. That meant a lot of driving from Austin early in the morning. He drove back to Austin that evening preparing to tell Skip about the situation and the crazy man from Dallas who was now in his company. He wondered what was going on in the Army to accept such a disturbed man for military service.

He thought that it could either mean the acceptance standards were very low, or the war in Europe was more serious than the government was telling the public, or a combination of the two realities. So, in the first day he had been confronted with a serious lack of equipment preparedness and questionable personnel standards in the Army. During the drive back to Austin, he was pensive and reflective as he tried to absorb the absurdity of the situation.

The next day Art made arrangements to meet the battalion executive officer which was important because he would be his immediate superior officer and his link to the battalion commander. He met the executive officer of the 1st Battalion in the parking lot of the A Company barracks. He parked the Dodge next to his jeep and waited for the meeting. Shortly, a black coupe pulled into the parking lot. It was a 1941 Lincoln Zephyr, V-12 coupe, one of the most expensive cars of the time. A major got out of the car and introduced himself as Therle Hill. Major Hill didn't have much to say, other than he was also from Dallas, had a wife and children there, stayed at the BOQ (bachelor officers quarters) at Swift, and went home to Dallas quite frequently. Art could tell immediately that the major was fastidious in his uniform dress and personal habits, a true "spit and polish" officer. He appeared to be about the same age as Art and had been commissioned out of a military school in the eastern United States. When he left the meeting with Major Hill, the Major said as he was getting into the Zephyr, "You've got your work cut out for you lieutenant. These men don't know shit from Shinola." Art nodded his head in agreement as the Zephyr lurched in reverse and then sped off leaving two tracks of white dust on the road.

Major Hill didn't divulge much about himself as Art worked with him over the next several months. At the time, that was okay with Art. Art did learn that Major Hill was nicknamed "Zephyr" behind his back by most of the people at Camp Swift. The Lincoln Zephyr was the most obvious, recognized, and out of place vehicle in, probably, the entire Central Texas area. It was a very fancy, black, and unmistakable automobile. Very few people could afford such a luxury vehicle, and it tended to draw attention. Over a period of time, Art noticed some unusual things about the major. The major kept a closed jar of alcohol on the front seat of the Zephyr so that he could wipe off the steering wheel if anybody had left germs on it when they drove the car. Major Hill had also placed a small blanket on the driver's side floorboard to keep the car clean. Finally, he also kept a pair of house slippers in the car that he could wear when he was driving. When he left the Zephyr, the slippers were placed on the ground under the driver's side and then retrieved when he got back in the car. Art was amazed and puzzled by such strange habits, but too busy to spend much time analyzing the observations.

Art put the company through basic training over the next few months as second lieutenants arrived to take over as platoon leaders in the company. At first, the inductees were ordered through calisthenics and a grueling obstacle course. Later, the platoons divided and trained at the rifle, pistol, bayonet, machine gun, mortar, and artillery ranges. In addition, the platoons would go to the bank of the Colorado River to practice "river crossings" and construction of pontoon bridges. During the training, the Texas heat was oppressive, so the river was a welcome, favorite, and anticipated assignment for the troops because they could cool off in the river. The camp didn't have a swimming pool at this time, but one was built later.

As the training continued, construction continued at a frantic war mobilization pace. Men and materiel poured into Camp Swift. More barracks and a chapel were completed. Many of the tar paper buildings were being covered in wooden white siding, so that the whole camp shimmered white in the summer Texas sun. The temperature in the daytime rose to over one hundred degrees and stayed there for days. The barracks absorbed the heat, and the inside of the barracks were like an oven with minimal ventilation. It took the buildings a long time to cool at night, so that the men were very uncomfortable sleeping at night, especially the trainees from the northern part of the country. They learned that Texas was hot and humid in the daytime and sultry at night. All of the windows stayed open. If the men hadn't been so exhausted from training in the oppressive heat, they would probably have had difficulty sleeping at night. Construction of a service club and gymnasium was started as more and more troops arrived for training. Many other smaller structures were under construction, and their use hadn't been announced by headquarters.

Art quickly discovered the arrangement that the camp had for troops to get to Austin. After a hot, dusty, and dry week of training, most of the troops were eager to get to Austin and socialize in a variety of establishments. Kerville Bus Lines had seventeen busses a day that shuttled between the camp and Austin. The soldiers got a free ride back from Austin on a six-by-six Army truck, but to get to Austin, they had to pay for the trip. When the troops arrived in Austin, they would visit Scholz's Garden, Pike's Place, Jacoby's, The Scoot Inn, or Tony's Tavern. A sign on the front of Tony's read "Let our defense blonds serve you." One of the saloons featured an alligator pit and badger fights. Most of the famous and numerous German beer gardens and houses of prostitution that flourished on the east side of Austin around the turn of the twentieth century had been the victims of prohibition. The influx of troops at the beginning of the war years provided a brief rebirth of Austin nightlife. Of course, the soldiers visited all of the available prostitutes in Austin that were now working as part of the entertainment rebirth. Like in other wars, many prostitutes had moved to the area to establish their "businesses." When the troops deployed to other camps or overseas, most of the popular madams and drinking establishments quickly faded away.

Moving troops around inside the camp soon became a major problem. As a solution, the camp contracted with the Bowen Bus Company. They used tractor trucks with very long trailers that could carry as many as two hundred soldiers each trip through the camp. These were open air trailers, and when it rained, the soldiers got wet and cold. The soldiers unaffectionately called them the "hog haulers," or "Bowen's buggies."

The highway between Austin and Bastrop, that Art continued to endure, was congested, and traffic moved slowly. The overworked, over-patched, and rationed tires on the busses frequently blew out and left stranded soldiers all along the highway. The soldiers hitchhiked the rest of the way to Austin—local residents frequently gave them a ride the rest of the way to Austin. The military police six-by-six trucks continued to stay busy bringing troops back to the camp who got into legal trouble in Austin.

Art gradually developed good working relationships with his superior officers, including most of the cadre who came from Fort Sam Houston to open the camp, the camp executive officer who was also the Lieutenant Colonel in charge of all the ranges, the major who was the quartermaster, the Lieutenant Colonel who was supervising construction, the division artillery officer who was a Brigadier General, and the chief medical officer.

He also developed good working relationships with his subordinate officers in the company when they arrived to take over duties in the company. He prized these relationships. They made his job much easier and less anxiety producing in a situation where it was easy to have a lot of confusion, conflict, and control problems relating to command overlap, inconsistencies, gaps, and ambiguity.

Art slowly became more suspicious and wary of Major Hill, the battalion executive officer. At first, he was mildly uncomfortable with his cold and closed personality along with his "spit and polish" appearance and personal habits. Major Hill's uniforms were always creased in a particular way with three vertical creases on the back of his shirts. All of his uniforms were private purchases instead of being issued by the Army. His superficial conclusion about the major was that he was wealthy or came from a wealthy family. Art considered that the major was just snobbish, conceited, very eccentric, pseudoaristocratic, or a "kiss ass." He thought about it as he continued to have limited contact with the major over weeks of training, but the major hadn't caused him any direct or indirect grief that he was aware of, so the discomfort stayed in the back of his mind.

Across the entire camp, no one knew much about the very aloof major. He seemed to be distant and disconnected with most of the other people in the camp.

The first substantial realization that increased his suspicion concerned Major Hill's trips home to Dallas when the major had a weekend or three-day pass. After hearing Major Hill declare his intentions and then observing his departures, Art strongly suspected that the major wasn't truthful about where he was going. First, Dallas was, at least, a six hour trip and the major was never packed for such a long trip.

Second, the major never seemed to be concerned about obtaining enough gas for the trip, and he never seemed to have much gas in the Zephyr. Finally, on one occasion, the major was in the camp when he claimed to have been in Dallas. He couldn't have gone to Dallas and returned in the short time he said he was gone from the camp.

Art let his suspicions rest for awhile. He had to be very cautious. A superior officer could make his life miserable in the military command fishbowl he was in if he made the officer his enemy, not to mention getting poor performance ratings. Most important, he didn't want his suspicions to ruin his military career. It was a question of whether he could trust the major.

Finally, Art asked an MP, who he had gotten to know quite well, and a man he thought he could trust to not tell anyone about Art's question concerning where Major Hill went when he left the camp. At first the MP was understandably hesitant to divulge any dope about such a high-ranking officer. Art continued to press the MP for information.

Finally, the MP told him that Major Hill went to Austin when he got a pass and had been seen frequently at Barton Springs and Zilker Park. He said that the Zephyr had been seen quite often around the park. He said that Major Hill had gotten into some "trouble" in Austin, but he refused to provide any details or more information. Art didn't press for any more information. He had heard enough to decide to direct his next inquiry to a different source.

The training of A Company continued through the oppressive dust and heat of the late summer months of 1942. Art had managed to scrounge a few items of field equipment, including a sun helmet that was allowed for officers to wear. The firing ranges were expanded to two ranges of seventy five targets each and one range of one hundred targets. The ranges were a distance of one hundred yards, two hundred yards, three hundred yards, and five hundred yards.

The artillery range was set up so that firing could be made in excess of six miles. A Company spent a lot of time on the ranges as the camp grew larger from inductees arriving at the camp from all over the country.

After three weeks of driving to the camp from Austin, Art and Skip made the decision to move to Bastrop. The early mornings at the stockade had become a chronic problem, in addition to the highway between the cities becoming more congested. He also found that he was expected to stay in the barracks at the camp for periods of two to three weeks before he could get a leave of absence. The temperature in Central Texas was extremely high, the soldiers in all of the barracks were bored and stressed, and the barracks were confining, so officers were increasingly required to stay in the barracks to maintain control, reduce conflicts between the men, and diffuse potential interpersonal confrontations. Fights were frequent as the oppressive heat got on the soldier's nerves. They learned to be more aggressive from their training. Art had a private room in the barracks where he slept on an Army bunk. He ate with the company in the camp mess hall, so he cherished Skip's cooking and a softer bed when he could get away from the camp.

Art reluctantly rented a two-car garage apartment in Bastrop, and the family moved closer to the camp. The apartment was small and primitive. It had a creaky wooden floor covered with linoleum, a bed, a refrigerator, and a stove in the same room. Their son slept on a canvass and wood Army cot in the same room. Skip was thankful that it had an adequate clothesline in the backyard and a wringer washer on the back porch. She anticipated she might have to wash clothes in the rain. The apartment was cramped, but its location meant that Art and Skip could spend more time together and Art's drive would be much shorter. The family spent free time at Bastrop State Park or cooling off by wading and swimming in the Colorado River and the state park swimming pool. The river was a refreshing experience of cool, clear water in a hot Texas summer, unlike the muddy and inaccessible rivers of the Dallas area.

Art rented the one room apartment from Mrs. Marjorie Van Valkenburg, an elderly widow. Mrs. Van Valkenburg's husband had been a WW 1 veteran, so she was one of the few local people who were sympathetic toward military families.

Mrs. Van Valkenburg employed a black maid named Eula Johnson. Her ancestors had been brought up the Colorado River as slaves to work in the plantation houses and on the plantation farms in the river bottom lands. They came on the steamboat *Kate Ward* from Galveston and Matagorda. Eula walked every day, to work for the landlady, from the south side of Bastrop.

Art and Skip were very comfortable with the choice of the apartment. It was in a safe neighborhood and the landlady was very hospitable and cordial. In Austin, they had a private back yard, which they did not have now. In addition, there were soldiers living all over the small town, especially on the weekends. But, under the circumstances, they felt safe and secure in the less private location of the new apartment. Their son rode his tricycle on the sidewalk next to the big house and around the goldfish pond that had been built around two large pecan trees in the back yard. He watched the school children walking to school and coming home from school. The closest neighbor child was a girl who lived in the next block. He watched as she and her friends walked home from school. There weren't any children his age to play with, so he was fascinated with the older children as they walked home from school.

Art and Skip soon learned that some of the local people scolded and criticized the landlady for renting to "Army people." The family would soon find out that they underestimated the depth of the resentment directed toward military families. Thousands of uprooted soldiers and their families were suddenly cast into a small town of deeply rooted civilians as a result of war mobilization. They were a kind of reverse war refugee. Instead of running from a war-torn area, they had run toward a town that led to a war area. It was a truly transitional culture clash that all the parties involved hoped would end quickly. Unfortunately, local citizens, who stayed informed about the wars raging in the Pacific and European areas, were not as optimistic as less informed citizens. Their feelings were influenced by a general sense of anxiety and dread. They sensed the scope of what the country was headed for on the other side of two oceans. They were caught in a conflict between strong patriotism and personal discomfort.

Shortly after Art and Skip rented the garage apartment, Mrs. Van Valkenburg started renting cots in the second floor of the big house. Soldiers who rented the cots were ones who had enough money to rent a space in town, so that when they had a leave from Camp Swift, they had a place to go other than back to the barracks. Many times, when they came in late at night, their friends, who didn't have a place to sleep, simply slept in the front yard of the big house. Frequently, they left in a hurry, or half, leaving behind their leather Army jackets in the front yard. Mrs. Van Valkenburg would gather them and wait for the soldiers to retrieve their jackets when they came back.

The town soon became more comfortable with soldiers in local homes and in the community. Art was relieved that Private Clemmons wasn't one of her renters, but he didn't expect him to be, because he knew the man was quite poor before the war.

Art drove the Dodge back to Austin ostensibly to buy a tire. Finding tires for cars was a continuous quest, and the Dodge needed at least one newer tire. But, the primary reason for the trip was to go to a Western Union Telegraph Office. He found a telegraph office and sent six telegrams to grocery salesmen he knew in Dallas while he was working there as a salesman, including Bill Buchan. All six telegrams had the same wording:

URGENT. NEED INFORMATION ON THERLE HILL OF DALLAS. NO NAMES ON REPLY.

All six telegrams went out from the Austin office. Art knew he couldn't risk sending them from the one office in Bastrop or the office at the camp headquarters. Telegraph operators on both ends of the connection could read the telegram and he didn't want anybody in Bastrop or the camp aware of his inquiry. He told the office in Austin to hold any replies and he would come back periodically to see if there were any replies.

Art went by the office the next weekend to see if there were any return telegrams. There was one and it read:

H & H GROC CO.

"Well I'll be damned," Art exclaimed out loud.

"I should have recognized that," he followed up.

H & H Grocery Company was a well known wholesale grocery company in Dallas. The "H & H" stood for Hill and Harlan, the owners of the company. Art knew the Hill family lived in Highland Park, an incorporated city on the northwest edge of Dallas. He also knew they were very wealthy. So, he concluded that Major Hill was one of the children of the original owner. Most grocery salesmen in Dallas knew about H & H because they made sales calls to keep the warehouses stocked with whatever product or line of products they represented. Art had been to the H & H warehouse many times and had met owner "Red" Hill on several occasions.

He never had any occasion to know about the man's family, and the owner never mentioned he had a son in the military, which now seemed very strange to Art, because most people were very proud of family members in the military and they took advantage of any situation to talk about them. Art remembered that he had mentioned several times to the owner that he was an officer in the Army Reserve.

He went back to the telegraph office in Austin a week later and didn't find any replies to his original request. He waited another week and hit the jackpot. The office had a telegram from Buchan, his close, but brief golfing friend in Dallas.

He opened the telegram and it read:

ARRESTED FOR MOLESTING A 12 YEAR OLD CHILD OF A FAMILY FRIEND. HUSHED UP. SENT TO CEDARLAWN PSY HOSP FOR 6 MONTHS. SENT THEN TO MILITARY SCHOOL OUT OF STATE.

"Shit," Art cursed out loud. He was stunned at first and then became angry and shocked.

"A major, for God's sake. What-tha-hell's going on here?" he asked himself. "No wonder his father hadn't mentioned his son."

He stood outside the telegraph office with the telegram folded up. He looked up at the sky and then down at the folded paper for a few minutes. This was more than he was prepared for, but it confirmed his earlier suspicions about Major Hill.

He said in almost a whisper, "This man is not just an oddball, but a bad egg and the Army has to know about it."

Art realized that he had walked right into a potentially volatile, touchy, and toxic situation. He didn't know what to do with the information other than to watch the major closely and give him a wide berth. He remembered that Cedarlawn Psychiatric Hospital was well known in the Dallas area. It was the place where the rich people in the city and surrounding areas went when they had mental, drinking, or drug abuse problems. Publicly and politically, the reason most often given for their hospitalization was "nervous breakdown." In reality, they were sent there for a variety of rarely disclosed reasons.

Art wasn't sure whether he would tell Skip what Buchan had communicated in his telegram. He thought about it on the way home to Bastrop. He told her when he got back to the apartment. They agreed to not say anything to anybody about what the telegram said, but the information increased the overall anxiety level of the assignment to Camp Swift. He was thankful that Skip had a keen sense of knowing what to do in stressful situations and he relied on her support. Art now had an unstable soldier in his company and an immediate superior officer with a history of mental problems.

He and Skip hoped that everyone involved, especially Art, would be trained and deployed before anything bizarre happened at Camp Swift. At the end of August, 1942, Art was unexpectedly switched from commanding officer of A Company to B Company and immediately received a notice that he was appointed "Class A, Agent Finance Officer" for the Disbursing Officer for the 95th Infantry Division to make cash payments to the men of B Company. A new captain had arrived at the camp and assumed command of A Company.

The training of A and B Companies progressed into the fall of 1942. The training routine was grueling. It consisted of push-ups, calisthenics, hand-to-hand bayonet drills, "dirty fighting" classes, close order drills, map reading, night patrols, night maneuvers, machine gun and barbed wire course, two runs over the full combat courses every day, a thirty two mile forced march, a ten mile speed march, and a two mile double time march. All marches were conducted with trainees outfitted with full winter field equipment, three days of rations, an overcoat, extra boots, a rifle, and a bayonet. Art was getting more confident that the company was getting into top fighting shape. The men were getting physically fit, and their fighting skills were at a high level of proficiency. Their readiness was his responsibility, and he felt he had done his job as a company commander. The temperatures in south central Texas were still unbearably high as the troops continued to get into combat and physical readiness. They continued to socialize in Austin on the weekends, but they didn't have much difficulty sleeping at night after the training exercises. The MPs continued to transport some troops back to the stockade.

Art continued to get soldiers out of the stockade. The camp continued to grow to over two thousand buildings. For a while, for Art, the routine was free of any serious personnel problems. With the varied age and maturity levels of men in his company, Art still had continuous minor personnel problems. As the company commander, he was aware of most of these minor problems. He knew there were some he didn't hear about and preferred to not know about them as long as the problem didn't disrupt training or result in a serious health threat.

Some of the men had psychological problems. Others had physical problems. Art had trainees who sleepwalked around the barracks at night. Some went out the door of the building. He knew about men who cried at night. They were young and had never been away from home for any length of time. They were lonely and scared. Some of the men screamed from nightmares at night. Others screamed from leg cramps. At one point, there was an outbreak of dysentery or GIs in the barracks. Several men snored at a level that disturbed the sleep of other men. He even had one young trainee who wet the bed. He had men in the hospital for treatment of minor cuts, scrapes, contusions, or blisters on their feet. One was being treated for hives. So, minor medical and psychological problems kept him busy night and day during training. Finally, Art detected the other men in the company had began to notice Private Clemmons' strange behavior. The other trainees didn't openly say anything about their observations. From their nonverbal communication, Art could tell they knew something wasn't quite right with Private Clemmons' behavior. They would roll their eyes, smirk, grin, or nod their heads to the right or left when they were communicating with each other about Private Clemmons. The focus of their nonverbal signals to each other had slowly become the "elephant in the living room" that everyone was aware of, but didn't talk about. Art didn't like the way social relations were developing around Private Clemmons, but he wasn't ready or able, at this time, to do anything about the situation.

In September, the entire company was wearing new combat boots, which were actually heavy leather high top shoes. Over the new boots, canvass ankle leggings were worn. Most of the soldiers hated the leggings because they took so much time to lace up and unlace after pant legs were tucked in the top of the leggings. The company still did not have any rifles. Art began to think that the absence of rifles was a blessing, because he wasn't completely sure that the men wouldn't shoot or hit each other with them and there was at least one man in the company that Art felt very uncomfortable with the prospect of the man having a rifle.

After a few visits to the shooting ranges, it didn't take very long for most of the camp to realize that Art had a distinct advantage over most of the officers and enlisted men. He was an expert marksman with both a pistol and a rifle. Not only did he shoot on his college ROTC rifle team, but also won medals, trophies, and awards at the Austin, Dallas, and Georgia pistol and rifle clubs. The understanding around the camp was that Captain Shafer could "hit a gnat's ass at one hundred yards." The men in A and B Companies knew about his skills. He expected the men to be crack shots, so the company spent a lot of time on the shooting ranges.

In September, four months after his arrival at Camp Swift, Art received a notice that his personal equipment had arrived. The following list is what he received and signed for:

| | | | | |
|---|---|---|---|---|
| 1 | Helmet, M1 | 1 | fork M10 |
| 1 | Bag, field canvas | 1 | spoon M10 |
| 1 | Pistol Belt | 1 | pouch 1st. Aid |
| 2 | Blankets, WOD | 1 | packet 1st. Aid |
| 1 | canteen | 1 | suspenders belt cart |
| 1 | cover canteen | 1 | gas mask |
| 1 | cup canteen | 2 | shelter halves |
| 1 | can meat | 10 | pins tent shelter halves |
| 1 | knife M10 | 2 | poles, TSH |
| 1 | belt, cart cal. .30. | | |

The helmet looked new and unused, but the rest of the equipment was First World War surplus and dated 1917 and 1918. Art needed some binoculars, a field compass, and a map case, so he continued to search and scrounge for the items he needed and items officers were expected to have to train the soldiers.

Art owned a 38 caliber revolver and a 45 caliber pistol that he used in competition shooting in Dallas before the war and at Fort Benning. He expected to be issued a side arm or a carbine at Camp Swift, but he wasn't.

# Chapter 4

## Skip and the Sock Monkey

The limbs on the large pecan trees along the major streets of Bastrop hung low to the ground, heavy with pecan clusters. Most of the life sustaining nuts would fall by Thanksgiving, but for now they were safe from marauding crows, hungry squirrels, and overly eager tree thrashers. The coveted nuts had been sustaining Native Americans for thousands of years when they made a pilgrimage to the groves for the annual harvest on the banks of the Colorado River in Texas. Early European settlers wisely realized the value of the nutrients in the flavorful nuts and cultivated and protected the trees all over Central Texas. When early settlers arrived, there were dimpled and concave nutting, grinding, and cracking stones left by the first Americans, still scattered under the trees.

Skip pulled the red wagon, loaded with groceries and her son, back toward the apartment along the side of Water Street under the pecan trees. She was returning from the commercial district west of the courthouse. The apartment was located in a community north of the courthouse that was dotted with Greek Revival, Queen Ann, neoclassical, and Victorian style homes. Art and Skip were very familiar with the old southern homes after spending time in Georgia and driving the avenues, lined with old homes, stretching north from downtown Dallas. Skip could tell the converted double garage on Water Street was the smallest dwelling in the neighborhood and similar to other detached garages built next to the large homes after automobiles arrived on the scene. Art and Skip thought it was humorous that the original sets of parallel tire ruts led up to the front of the building and abruptly stopped where the front of the garage had been enclosed. The apartment had originally been built for the Van Valkenburg's Model T or Model A Ford cars. It was also detached from the main house which was built before 1900.

Mrs. Van Valkenburg's house was a large white Queen Ann style home with fretwork and gingerbread exterior appointments. The metal fretwork had been brought from a German ornamental ironworks in Austin. The fretwork was added several years after the home had been built. Now, the landlady was having a difficult time keeping up such a big house and paying bills. The rental income from the garage apartment, and other rooms in the house, was a help to her. Skip had been to the post office and grocery store near the court house square. She had to allow for most of the day to get the errands done because there were usually long lines at both the post office and grocery store. Many items were rationed and the citizens of Bastrop were standing in line with many of the new military families.

In September, 1942, there were one hundred twenty-five officers, in addition to Art, at Camp Swift. The regimental commander, a colonel, and four lieutenant colonels lived in Austin. Four officers lived in Taylor, Texas, three in Elgin, Texas, three in Smithville, Texas, and one in Bryan, Texas. Two officers lived at Bastrop State Park. The rest lived in Bastrop, Austin, or the BOQ. Like Art, many officers had families with them. Many local citizens were unhappy with, reeling from, and shocked by military intrusion and congestion in their lives. They resented and were suspicious of the new arrivals. Skip quickly felt the resentment and hostility of local citizens. Local people wouldn't speak to her in stores, town, and church services. On occasion, they would cross the street to avoid passing her on the same side. Skip attended a Methodist church that she could walk to a couple of blocks from the house. Fortunately, the people in the church were cordial, friendly, and welcoming. Finally, Skip asked Mrs. Van Valkenburg about what was going on in the town. She learned from her that the resentment and hostility, she had experienced, sprang from several sources. First, the predominately German-American community attitudes about the war ranged from mild uneasiness to strong opposition. This attitude was typical of many communities in the United States whose citizens were first or second generation immigrants of German origin. Many had relatives in Germany, were members of German clubs in the community, still spoke German, still celebrated traditional holidays, like May Day, on the first day of May, and were descendents of "free thinkers" who had immigrated to Texas in the 1850s.

On the second level, the citizens of Bastrop had not only lost a once quiet and peaceful community, but also their bus station, telegraph office, utility services, grocery stores, post office, court house offices, and the small telephone service they once enjoyed, to hoards of "outsiders." Before Camp Swift, life had been orderly, peaceful, and comfortable, as long as black citizens "stayed in their place." Now they had the added anxiety about black soldiers being in the community with a new, but ambiguous, social status. Now, day to day tasks were chaotic, tedious, and undependable. The social currents of the community were also complicated by a love-hate relationship between the town and camp. Juxtaposed with the resentment toward the intrusion by the military was the opportunity for many local citizens in the city and region to conduct business with the camp. In addition to the large number of civilians working at the camp, many local entrepreneurs sold needed supplies to the camp, ranging from fresh vegetables to building supplies. As a result, the camp provided a significant economic boost to an otherwise economically stagnate region and insulated community. Economic times had been hard in Bastrop. Some people loved and welcomed the new money, but many people hated the military.

Finally, the community of Bastrop was tense, anxious, and fearful like many other small communities caught up in the mobilization for war. A war was raging in Europe and starting to engulf much of Asia. These small communities were previously fairly detached from developing events on the other side of the world. But now, the explosion of military activity overwhelmed the small town and created a reality about the urgency, commitment, and fear created by a declaration of war. Bastrop, like other communities, was stunned by the mobilization. War preparations were no longer remote from the Bastrop citizens. So, it was understandable that the community was not socially, economically, psychologically, or politically prepared for the drastic changes.

Skip grew up in a town the size of Bastrop, so she knew how a small town could resent outsiders. In her hometown, the citizens of German origin resented the citizens of Czech origin, and they both resented citizens of Native American origin. She knew very well. Her father was Czech; her mother was Native American.

Now, she was caught in the middle of local currents. The local citizens tended to show their thinly veiled resentments to military families. Art was gone for longer periods of time and was not as aware of, or a target of, local sentiments, so she relied on Mrs. Van Valkenburg to keep her informed about the social dynamics in the community. Fortunately, the landlady was both informative and protective. Skip was very isolated, vulnerable, and alienated in the community, so the landlady became her guardian angel, source of information, and only friend in the community. There wasn't a phone in the apartment, so she had to rely on the use of the one phone in the big house. Most people with phones were on "party lines," so many times Mrs. Van Valkenburg or Skip would have to wait to use the phone when other users were not on the line. The local phone services were overwhelmed by the addition of new residents.

In addition to taking care of her son, Skip spent most of her time doing laundry to keep Art clothed in clean and pressed khaki uniforms. She had to wash and starch the uniforms, hang them on an outside line, and then iron the shirts and pants.

The apartment wasn't designed for so much laundry. Art brought dirty uniforms home daily when he first arrived at Camp Swift. The camp had a laundry, but the turn-around time was too long, so he brought them home. Then, when he had to stay longer, the laundry procedure didn't work, so he had them done at the camp. About the time he got used to getting them done at the camp laundry, the camp decided to consolidate operations with Bergstrom Air Base. It was decided that Bergstrom would do all of the laundry for the two facilities, and Camp Swift would do all of the baking. As a result, the two military bases transported laundry and baked goods back and forth between them. For Art, it meant scrambling to get uniforms cleaned, and for Skip, it meant that she would get a week of dirty uniforms to clean and iron in two days time. Laundry remained chaotic at Camp Swift and in the small and poorly equipped apartment.

Now that Art was spending more time living at the barracks, Skip began to notice that Art's uniforms had the faint odor of a skunk. After three or four times noticing the odor, Skip asked Art about it. Art explained that skunks had invaded the crawl spaces under the barracks and the culverts under the streets. The soldiers chased them out, and the skunks only invaded another building. The more the soldiers harassed the skunks, the worse the smell became. If a skunk died under a building, the smell lingered for weeks at a time. Art admitted to Skip that skunks weren't the only problem they had with critters. The original noise and construction caused most of the critters that lived in the area, to flee to safer areas around the camp. Once the camp settled into a quieter routine, they quickly returned. Not only were the skunks leaving their pungent odor wafting through the barracks, but the raccoons were raiding the trash cans at the mess hall. Armadillos scurried around the camp like they owned the real estate when the sun went down. They dug and rooted all over the camp, looking for buried edible treasures. In the daytime, they disappeared into the many holes they had created.

In addition, the coyotes ran the fields of the camp at night, creating a ruckus with their high pitched yelps that sounded like twenty screaming babies. The coyotes scared the bejesus out of the "city boys" when the critters seemed to be directly outside the barracks. They got even more unnerved when the coyotes would all suddenly stop yelping at the same time and quiet would return. The "city boys" knew the coyotes were still near and very close to the barracks. There were some sleepless nights for some of the trainees until the training got more grueling, and their exhaustion caused them to sleep without any interruption from local critters. Art and Skip laughed about the Army being at war with the skunks and other critters at Camp Swift.

Skip became the paperwork executive for all of Art's dealings with the Army bureaucracy. Documentation was extensive for Art because each commanding officer was responsible for all company property, both in the mess hall and barracks. All personal items and company property had to be inventoried, recorded, and returned whenever an officer was transferred to another assignment or a battalion relocated. While Art was at Camp Swift, there was a lot of movement of men in and out of the camp as the company mobilized for war. This movement created an accompanying volume of paper documentation and recording of Army property. Skip had to keep precise records because if an item couldn't be accounted for, they would have to pay for it. Art's pay was $166 a month plus $60 for rental allowance and $37 for food, and they didn't want any additional expenses.

The first red tape, rigmarole, and paper mix-up occurred shortly after Art had arrived at Camp Swift in June. Art and Skip were living in Austin. The Regimental Command officer for the 379th Regiment, a Major Sarham, asked Art to go to the Sherwin Williams store in Austin and purchase painting supplies to refinish the desks in the headquarters offices. This caused a paperwork mix-up that lasted until August. Art got caught between the major, a captain who was the regimental supply officer, and the Sherwin Williams store in Austin. It wasn't clear who was supposed to pay for the varnish, sandpaper, brushes, and turpentine. The major had given Art money to purchase the supplies which Art did purchase. The major found he didn't have enough paint, so he sent Art to the store again. To get his money back for the supplies, he had to go through the regimental supply officer. The major didn't get paid until August. In the meantime, Sherwin Williams was billing Art for the second list of supplies. Skip made sure she kept a record of all of the mixed-up paperwork, so that Art didn't have to pay for the paint.

Shortly after the first of September, Skip was returning from one of her regular trips to the grocery store, and as she neared the apartment, she noticed a difference in the sky to the southeast. The sky was dark, cloudy, and foreboding all across the horizon. She had never seen this weather phenomenon before, but she had heard people talk about it in southern Georgia. She was familiar with storms approaching from the northwest, but not from the southeastern direction. She increased her pace back to the apartment and went to see Mrs. Van Valkenberg. The landlady had been listening to the radio, and she told Skip that a hurricane was approaching. Skip was astounded and fearful of what to expect from the storm. The landlady said that the storm had come from the Gulf of Mexico and was now spinning northward through Central Texas. She was worried that it could be a bad storm. She said she was worried because she was descended from ancestors that died in the hurricane that had destroyed Galveston forty years earlier.

Both of the women began rushing around to prepare for the storm. Skip didn't know what to do to prepare for the storm. Nobody else seemed to know either when she asked the neighbors who came out of the houses next door and from across the street. Art was at the camp, so she was on her own to protect herself and her son. She didn't have much time to worry about what was going to happen because the wind started blowing, and the big pecan trees started swaying as dust and debris blew through the neighborhood. Then the rain came. Bands of heavy rain lashed the small apartment, first in one direction and then in the opposite direction. Skip couldn't see anything through the windows. The downpour lasted for hours, and then she began to see the streets and yards when the rain subsided and the sky got brighter. There were broken tree limbs scattered everywhere. The streets and yards were flooding, and the water was rising around all of the houses. It looked to her like the neighborhood had become a lake. And, then she noticed that water was coming in through the front and back doors. The apartment was flooding, so she started getting as many things off the linoleum floor as possible.

The entire small garage apartment flooded. All she could do was to hold her son and sit on a table as the water rose to a level about six inches deep. She was stuck, scared, and alone. She was especially worried that the water would continue to rise. She didn't have any way to contact anybody. It was getting dark outside, and she was also worried about spending the night in the flooded apartment with the threat of fire from an electrical malfunction. She thought how ironic it was that they lived on Water Street. After about two hours of sitting on the table, the rain stopped, and she saw the light from a car's headlights flash across and illuminate the front windows of the apartment. The front door opened creating a small wake in the water in the apartment. It was Art who had arrived in a Jeep. He had driven in the storm from the camp, and he was soaking wet. Skip was crying, and Art's face was pale as his eyes flashed around in fear as he looked over the perilous scene.

Art and Skip enjoyed a cold, wet, and brief embrace as they stood in the calf-deep flood water. They grabbed some dry clothes and towels and headed for the Mina Hotel in the center of town. All of the streets were flooded, but the Jeep went right through the inundation. It was a cold Jeep ride. It took several days for the water, on Water Street and other streets, to recede and for the city to clean up the mess blocking the streets. Mrs. Van Valkenburg told them that the surrounding creeks and Colorado River bottoms had flooded, and many people had been evacuated into the city. Art and Skip discovered they were victims of a major drainage problem in the small town. The town was well above the level of the Colorado River, so the threat of direct flooding from the river was remote. On the other hand, the town was located on a low-lying plain above the river with almost no formal drainage system. Fortunately, the big house was constructed two feet above the ground on piers and beams, so it was not affected by the rising water.

In addition to not having any sidewalks, the town did not have curbs, gutters, or storm drains; consequently, in the neighborhoods surrounding the town square, the water from heavy rains was impounded in the town on rare occasions. Many structures in the neighborhoods were flooded. In later years the city's solution was to raise the level of the homes instead of improving the drainage.

Skip had endured and survived her first hurricane, and she didn't even live near the Gulf coast. Central Texas, Bastrop, and Camp Swift quickly dried when the late summer heat returned. The small apartment didn't smell too bad from the flood, but Skip kept it open whenever she could so that mold and mildew didn't create an unpleasant smell. She scrubbed everything in the apartment with a bleach solution and soon her routine returned to normal. The only casualty of the flood was the floor of the apartment. The wooden floorboards under the linoleum warped even worse than they had been, so that the family now had a corduroy floor.

Art went back to the camp and was gone for two weeks. The town didn't have a sewer system, so all of the septic tanks behind the houses flooded. Now, there was a distinct sewage odor in the neighborhood. It took two weeks to dissipate. The pumping trucks were busy for a week cleaning up the mess left by the flooded tanks. A truck eventually came and pumped the tank behind the apartment, so that Skip could run the water, flush the toilet, and continue to wash their clothes.

After Skip had telephoned her mother in Iowa, she received a letter from her. Her mother said in the letter that she didn't hear much of the phone conversation because of the poor reception. The letter expressed her mother's "blues" from missing her daughter and husband, Skip's father. He was away from home in Rochester, Minnesota for treatment for bladder and prostate cancer. He went there many times for surgery until the cancer finally killed him years after the war was over. Her mother didn't drive a car, and she mentioned it was zero degrees outside, but Skip's younger brother kept her company. The cost of a hotel room near the hospital was fifteen dollars a night, so the high cost of the room made her decide to stay home. She mentioned that she sent Skip's father a carton of Kool cigarettes. She also expressed worry about her sons leaving for war. Skip could tell the situation was difficult for her.

On the Friday morning before Art was scheduled to return for a weekend pass, the sirens at the Bastrop fire station started blowing nonstop for at least thirty minutes. Many of the residents in the neighborhood, where the apartment was located, walked into the streets to see what was burning. It didn't seem to Skip that anything was burning as she looked for smoke in all directions, but she knew there was a big fire somewhere. She guessed it was a barn on a farm outside of town because in Iowa, barns on the local farms burned occasionally and created big fires.

Art returned later than usual from the camp. He came in the apartment and sat on the bed. Skip could tell he was exhausted and dejected. He smelled of smoke.

"What happened, hon? What burned?" Skip asked.

"A warehouse burned," Art said.

"What?" Skip asked.

"Yea, the mattress warehouse burned and destroyed over one hundred and twenty-five thousand mattresses that were to be issued to the camp," Art replied.

Skip just stood there and didn't know what to say. She knew it was an enormous setback for the camp, and Art's body language communicated the loss. The loss of the mattresses would place a lot of pressure on the supplier and manufacturer. Before the fire, the problem of the beds the men slept on had been a headache for Art. His men slept on folding cots, bunk beds from World War 1, and metal hospital beds. Most had been scrounged from other locations, mostly from military installations in San Antonio, and hastily trucked to Camp Swift. Many were broken and damaged.

For Art, it meant that many of his current soldiers and many yet to arrive would have to continue to sleep with only blankets on steel mesh springs.

"The fire was in warehouse number 11 and it was too intense and hot to get mattresses out of the warehouse that were undamaged. We couldn't get trucks close to the warehouse. All we could do was watch it burn," Art recalled with a helpless tone of voice and a blank look on his face.

A board of inquiry later determined that the fire was caused by stacking the mattresses too high, so that they were too close to the two hundred watt lamps which were the primary lights in the warehouse. The hot lights heated the mattresses, and they ignited.

"This is a helluva kettle of fish," Art declared in reference to the Camp Swift situation.

After getting cleaned up from the fire and using his weekend pass to be with the family, Art went back to Camp Swift to confront the mattress losses. Two weeks passed, and Art returned to the apartment. Another crisis had occurred at the camp.

Several artillery shells had landed, not only outside the designated impact area, but also outside the boundaries of the entire Camp Swift reservation. Civilians living on farms were in obvious extreme danger, and they were angry and frightened. The Army downplayed the occurrences, but Art and the rest of the officers knew that it happened more than officials stated publically. What Art and others did not realize was the extent of the environmental hazard that unexploded ordinance created after the camp was closed, and much of the land was returned to agricultural uses by the original owners.

Shortly after the ordinance crisis, a motor repair shop was destroyed by fire. About thirty trucks that were in the shop for repairs were destroyed. One crisis after another led Art and Skip to the conclusion they were in a very chaotic situation. In the middle of the month of October, Skip was again returning to the apartment with the wagon loaded with groceries.

About a block from the apartment, she saw Mrs. Van Valkenberg standing outside of the small apartment. Skip hurried to her to see the cause for the landlady's concern. As Skip neared, she could see the lady was distraught and frightened. She was waving her arms to get Skip to come quickly.

"Get inside," the landlady directed. "Quickly."

"What happened?" Skip asked.

"Oh, it's terrible," she replied, closing the door behind Skip. "An MP killed a nigra soldier. There could be a lot of trouble."

"Oh no," Skip replied

"Yes..........yes...........Oh my god," Mrs. Van Valkenberg stuttered as she began to shake and hyperventilate.

"There's talk in town of a race riot and big trouble from the nigras," she added.

Skip didn't leave until Art came home from the camp. When he did arrive, he had heard about all the rumors about the shooting. The various rumors were divided by racial lines. The most consistent story was that a white MP shot and killed a colored soldier in a "juke joint" in southeastern Bastrop called "Charlie's Playhouse." The colored soldier was a member of a band that played at dances at the service club at Camp Swift. There was widespread fear in the Bastrop community that the "niggers" would start a race riot. Of course, any public protest by colored citizens would be considered a race riot by white citizens and handled accordingly. Letters were sent from the "Black KKK" to the Bastrop newspaper and the judge threatening retaliation for the killing of the soldier. In the meantime, the heightened fear and anger in the two communities simmered and festered. All of the citizens in the small town knew the anger about the incident wasn't over, and it had not been forgotten.

The shooting of the black musician was a sample of violence toward black soldiers, especially musicians, across the Jim Crow south in basic training camps. Most of the white musicians in the country had been drafted and were serving in combat positions. Black Americans served, not by choice, in noncombat positions and on a strictly segregated basis. Blood supplies for saving the lives of the wounded were carefully separated by race. Camp Swift had a schedule of separate services for "Catholics, Jews, Protestants, and Negros." Bastrop and Austin were fully segregated.

This included schools, restaurants, hotels, train cars, waiting rooms, public restrooms, hospitals, cemeteries, swimming pools, drinking fountains, jails, and churches. When the military services found they needed musicians for entertainment on the bases, the services turned to colored servicemen who had been musicians before the war.

Consequently, there was a colored band that played for white soldiers at Camp Swift. At Camp Swift, like other bases across the south, the colored musicians became racial targets for white MPs and white soldiers who objected to the musician's good clothes, hipster language, new assertiveness, and noncombatant status. The noncombatant status meant they were not likely to die or be wounded for their country. It was a racially volatile situation.

The black soldiers were keenly aware of the hypocrisy of being asked to fight bigotry abroad while experiencing it at home. Off the base, black soldiers were harassed, assaulted, and refused service at restaurants.

It wasn't clear to most white and black citizens in Bastrop what caused the killing of a black musician, or what the white MP was doing in a nightclub for black people. It was clear to everyone that the black citizens in the town and region were very angry about the incident. They had to be very cautious because it had only been ten years since lynching of black people had been rampant all over Texas.

None had occurred in Bastrop, but they occurred frequently in Central Texas, and one had just occurred in July in the northeastern corner of the state. There was talk of retaliation and revenge in the black community, but as weeks passed nothing occurred. The MP was given a General Court Martial in order to clear his record. The County Judge, W. S. Mason, who was also a Major in the Judge Advocate General's Office at Camp Swift, was a key player in the trial of the soldier. The MP was cleared of all charges. There continued to be trouble with the colored soldiers at Camp Swift, but a race riot did not occur.

Skip returned to her daily routine after a week passed, and it seemed okay for her to leave the apartment. Shortly after the shooting of the musician, Art came home and told Skip that he and some other soldiers from the company had been invited for dinner at Judge Mason's home in Bastrop. The invitation was part of a larger program at the camp to develop goodwill with the surrounding white community. Judge Mason had taken the lead in the goodwill programs. There were service clubs and guest houses for dependents of military personnel who visited soldiers. In addition, spouses could visit and dine with soldiers at the camp dining hall. Art's invitation was part of a specific program to dine in the home of citizens. Art was selected along with several trainees, including Private Clemmons and several officers, including Major Hill. They were scheduled to attend as a group at the judge's home.

Skip was pleased with the invitation, even though she wasn't included. Art was apprehensive about the selection of two of the visitors to the judge's home. Skip asked Art about the judge and his home, and Art indicated that the only thing he knew was that the judge had a twelve year old daughter.

Skip was finishing sewing together a sock monkey for her son, so she suggested that Art take the sock monkey to the girl as a gift. Making sock monkeys from boot socks had been a tradition in Skip's family for at least two generations that she knew about. They agreed that the gift would be a fine gesture, so they wrapped it, and Art took it to the little girl.

When Art returned from dinner, Skip was excited and curious to learn all the details of the event, especially the gift. Art gave her a detailed description of the events of the special evening at the judge's home. The home was large and beautifully appointed. The food was excellent. The judge's wife served fresh pork shops and German sausage along with fresh local vegetables, rye bread, and strudel. He explained to Skip that the judge's home was a two and a half story, white frame, Victorian home with a covered porch across the front of the house. It was located in the next block north of where they lived. He said that it looked like a lot of the old homes in Atlanta and Columbus, Georgia. When he arrived for dinner, there was an Army truck, the Zephyr, and other cars parked on the street in front of the home. The Army truck looked out-of-place, like a strange anachronism, and like an odd symbol of mobilization in the small, quaint community.

He told Skip the inside of the house was appointed with expensive area carpets, drapes, and furniture. Art noticed the extensive use of beveled glass in the windows, custom door hardware, very elaborate lighting fixtures, and large food platters and serving bowls. The dinner was served in the dining room with the guests seated at a large dining table. Two black maids worked in the kitchen and served the food. Art explained to Skip that the home and its furnishings indicated that the judge was a highly respected, widely known, prominent, wealthy, and upper class member of the community. Art used a familiar term he had heard in Dallas. He said the place was "high cotton."

Art and the other officers wore the winter service uniforms with the dark brown tunic and "pink" pants. The inductees wore khaki uniforms with Garrison Caps. At Major Hill's insistence, the khaki uniforms were precisely creased, pleated, and starched. They wore khaki web belts with polished brass roller buckles. Their Garrison Caps were tucked in and folded over the web belts during the meal. It was a spiffy group. Art observed that the meal was socially uncomfortable, but it was the best meal he had eaten since they left Iowa. All of the guest soldiers were well behaved, but most of the non commissioned officers didn't have much to say during the meal. Art thought they might have been overwhelmed with the lavish surroundings of the judge's home. He and the other officers carried most of the conversation during the meal, which was just fine with Art. He had been apprehensive about Private Clemmons saying anything during the dinner. Art remembered his conversations with the man in Dallas before the war.

Art was most impressed with the judge's daughter, Polly. She was very bright, articulate, well-mannered, precocious, and attractive. She helped her mother serve the soldiers and moved around the dining room, making conversation with all of the guests. Art could tell that she was the focus of the family and a very cherished child.

The evening at the judge's home was very stressful for Private Clemmons. Before the evening arrived, he was apprehensive, worried, and tense. He had never attended a dinner like this. He worried about his manners and whether he would do or say something stupid and embarrassing. He tried to figure a way to get out of the visit, but he didn't want to stand out, so he went.

During the dinner, he was frozen in gesture, posture, and speech. He was horrified, but emotionally aroused when he discovered a little girl was present. He watched everything, but didn't say anything. He was also mesmerized by the fine food, lavish interior decorations, and immense size of the home. He had never been in a large house like this one. He had seen them in Dallas, but never from the inside. He had always known on Deep Elm that he was poor, but the judge's home showed, even more, how much he had missed in his life. He realized that evening that he was a lot poorer than he ever knew he was.

After the visit, the enlisted men boarded Army trucks and returned to Camp Swift. Orvalee was relieved, but still bewildered by what he had seen. He tried to sleep that night, but the images of the judge, his daughter, particularly his daughter, made him dizzy as the thoughts, sights, smells, and conversations raced in his mind. She was so close, but he couldn't speak. Now, many years of social shyness and ineptness rose to a level of anger and rage at himself, girls, and society. The close encounter with the little girl brought all of his frustration, anger, and rage to a boiling point. Something he wanted was right next to him, and he was too frozen and paralyzed to even speak to her. The object of his obsession was physically close, but he was socially many miles away. His anger rose to a maniacal, explosive, and desperate level.

He sulked and brooded in the daytime and dreamed that night, and for several subsequent nights, about having sex with the girl. The dreams always involved assaulting the girl, but the situations and locations changed. One dream was a sexual encounter with her at the state fair livestock pens. Another occurred with Dallas Police officers watching silently. The context of the assaults always changed and included unusual sights and sounds that were part of the dream, including music he had listened to on Deep Elm. He had heard Blind Lemon Jefferson playing in clubs and bars on Deep Elm many times. He couldn't remember all of the lyrics or the exact lyrics, but he related to Blind Lemon's songs and the music stayed in his mind.

One song that he remembered was Blind Lemon's "Black Snake Moan," which started with:

*You ain't got no mamma now.*
*She told me late last night, you don't need no mamma now.*
*Black snake crawlin' in my room.*

Orvalee would awaken frightened and trembling after the violent dreams. He had experienced violent dreams in the past, particularly a disturbing dream about killing his mother. He deeply loved her, so the dream confused and frightened him. But, he hated what she did for money, the way she treated men, and the way men treated her. He had always been confused about how he fit into her relationships with men.

What frightened him the most, now that he was older, was his trouble separating his dreams and daydreams from reality. He sometimes thought that his dreams had actually occurred. His bizarre experiences when he was younger were now mixed together with his previous and current dreams.

Skip was anxious to hear about the sock monkey. Art said the girl was delighted when she opened the gift and she didn't put it down the rest of the evening. Toys were scarce during the war because raw materials were being directed to the war effort. This toy seemed to be immediately prized by the little girl. Skip was also more relaxed and less alienated that night because the fear in the community had subsided. She and Art had experienced something more like her memories of home before the war. They talked that evening about how nice it would be to have a daughter like Polly someday. Polly Mason slept that night with her new stuffed toy in her arms.

# CHAPTER 5

## AWOL

Art steered the Dodge into one of the parking spaces in front of A Company's barracks. When he did, a reflection of a black coupe flashed in his rear view mirror. It was Major Hill. He steered the Zephyr into the next space and parked beside the Dodge. He stepped out of the Zephyr and went around the car to say something to Art. He said to Art he wanted to borrow the Dodge to go to Austin. He said there wasn't enough gas in the Lincoln to get there and back. He needed to get more office supplies for the women working in the headquarters building. They had depleted the supply of typing and carbon paper. He added that he would leave the keys in his car.

Art didn't think very long about the request and replied to the major that it was okay with him. The Dodge, he added, had plenty of gas, which, of course, it did with the extra gas tank. Major Hill quickly got into the Dodge with the requisition forms and drove away.

For Art, there wasn't anything unusual about the request. Officers around the camp were very casual about loaning vehicles. Most knew their vehicles would be left behind when they were eventually deployed overseas. So, they only owned them for a short time. In addition, enlisted men frequently drove Jeeps when it wasn't authorized.

But nobody actually stole vehicles around Camp Swift, or it wasn't considered theft when soldiers left in a Jeep. Everybody understood that a Jeep would be very visible and easy to track down in a small Central Texas town if somebody actually stole it. So, restrictions on the use of Jeeps were very relaxed.

After a few minutes of reflection, Art became more annoyed with the request by Major Hill. He didn't mind the major using the Dodge to get more supplies, but it seemed Major Hill was chronically low on gas for his car. Art dismissed any underlying meaning of the request and accepted that it was just part of the eccentricity of the major. But he was still puzzled why Major Hill seemed to travel to Austin so frequently. The major seemed to take advantage of every opportunity to leave the camp to go to Austin. Art continued to be wary and suspicious of the major. Art got into his Jeep and drove to the small arms firing range to be with his men.

Private Clemmons sat cross-legged on the ground in the shade of a scrubby mesquite tree with other trainees. He was wearing an odd assortment of khaki fatigue clothes that added up to three layers of clothing. The other men were all taking care to avoid an active ant hill. It was hot and their fatigues were soaked with sweat. The mesquite tree didn't provide much shade from the sun. Yellow jackets were buzzing and cicadas were rattling their wings all across the grove of trees. The company had been to the range several times before, so the grass was worn thin from their returns to the same spot. The ants didn't seem to care who had been there. They stayed busy. Most of the birds had fled from the sound of rifle, machine gun, mortar, grenade, and artillery reports weeks ago.

He smoked a cigarette and lallygagged while he waited for his time on the firing range. The trainees in Company A were taking turns on the range. Like many of the other trainees, he had never fired a gun before he came to the firing range. Also, like the other trainees, he continued to close his eyes and flinch when he pulled the trigger on the rifle. The result was that he didn't hit the target that he didn't see. The range instructors were moving from man to man to reinforce the instructions they had given on how to properly fire the weapon. Two trainees already had bandages on their faces from getting too close to the weapon, while they were aiming, when it discharged, recoiled, and hit them in the face. The instructors worked at the range all day, and each group kept them busy trying to teach inductees to be marksmen. The range sergeants barked their orders with each firing session.

"Ready on the right?
Ready on the left?
Fire at will.
Cease firing."

They had to keep a sharp eye on the inductees, because there was always one man, sometimes more, who would wave the muzzle of the rifle around in all directions, endangering all of the other men on the range. When it happened, three or four instructors would converge on the trainee and scream at him to keep the muzzle of the rifle "downrange." Private Clemmons cringed at the thought of getting such a loud, intense, and angry tongue lashing. Try as he could, even in the most stable prone firing position, he couldn't keep the front sight of the rifle from waving from side to side. He rarely hit the target and got the sign of "Maggie's Drawers." A man in the firing pit below the targets would wave a cloth attached to a pole to signal misses. These pieces of cloth became known as "Maggie's Drawers."

The men were firing from the prone position. The noise from the long row of rifles on the range was deafening as the trainees fired the rounds. After each shot, they threw open the bolts to eject the spent rounds. The empty brass casings made a pinging sound when they were ejected from the chambers. He heard one or two reports from the rifles and then he heard:

"Whump, whump, whump…………whump, whump………… whump, whump, whump, whump, whump," when the entire range seemed to be erupting at the same time. Dust kicked up from the muzzle blasts of the rifles, and the brass casings began to litter the ground. And then, all of the firing stopped. The range became quiet for a few minutes as spotters in the firing pits down range and below the targets marked "hits and misses."

During the lull in the firing, the entire company heard a sharp crack of thunder in the distance to the south of the camp. A bolt of lightning had struck a pine tree in the state park. It was very close. No one had noticed a fast moving dark cloud coming toward them from the southwest direction. Lightning started cracking and striking across the flat plain of the camp as the violent weather headed for the rifle range. The strikes were getting closer. Art huddled with the platoon leaders to discuss the decision to head back to the barracks. An unwritten policy was to continue firing practice in the rain, but in the close groupings of the men, one strike could kill several men. The officers decided to load the men in the big open trucks and get them out of the storm. They gave the order to the sergeants who barked the orders: "Off your asses and on to your feet, out of the shade and into the heat."

The men gathered their equipment and started walking to the trucks.

"Double time! Double time! Get into the trucks you bunch of pecker-woods," the sergeants screamed at the trainees. When the men realized the concern about the lightening, they skedaddled into the big trucks in a more disorderly fashion than their departures had been. The company traveled back to the barracks during a driving rain.

Private Clemmons went into the barracks and went to his bunk bed and found a telegram laying on the blanket. It had been brought to the barracks by someone in the camp headquarters. He stood looking at the telegram for a long time. It was in an envelope, and he was hesitant to open it. He was fearful of opening it, because he knew it could have come from only one place and could only be about one person. He didn't know anyone except his mother. He finally opened the telegram and read it. It was brief and stated:

ANNE HADLEY DIED OCT 10, 1942

Orvalee started getting dizzy, faint, and panicky just as soon as he read the message. He dropped the telegram on the floor. The telegram didn't say who sent it or where his mother was buried. It had been sent four days earlier.

*You're a bastard, Orvalee. Your mother was a whore. You are evil and you are going to die for her sins. Run Orvalee, run. Get away or they will find out how wicked you are. You're next to die. Run!*

Private Orvalee Clemmons panicked as he sensed the aura of a coming seizure. He didn't want the other men to see him having a seizure, so he grabbed the telegram and ran from the barracks. He knew that many poorly educated people and some religious groups still believed that a seizure was confirmation that the person's body was occupied by evil spirits, or their soul was possessed by the devil. When he approached the parking lot, he decided to swipe a Jeep and drive somewhere to wait for the aura to pass, think by himself, and distance himself from critical eyes. The barracks made him anxious, so he wanted to get to a peaceful place. The Jeep wasn't in the parking lot. Instead, the Lincoln Zephyr was parked in the place the Jeep usually occupied, and it was the only vehicle in the parking lot. Orvalee was surprised, but excited and drawn to the shiny, black car. He was still very covetous of shiny, black coupes. He knew it belonged to the major, so he hesitated and stood by the driver's side of the fancy car. He doubled over in the agony of indecision. Take it. Don't take it. He looked in the car and saw that the keys were in the ignition. He was starting to get very wet from the rainstorm that followed the lightening storm. So, he opened the door, jumped in the driver's seat, started the Zephyr by turning the key, pushed the starter button on the dashboard, and drove away. He was immediately excited by the power and responsiveness of the large engine in the Zephyr. He had driven Jeeps and ice delivery trucks, but they were crude jalopies compared to the smooth force of the coupe.

Orvalee didn't know the area and didn't know where to go in his fancy new ride. He knew the route from the barracks to the river, so he headed the Zephyr toward the Colorado River. He turned off the paved road, crossed the railroad tracks, and headed for the river. The road was rough, but dry. The storm had missed the area of the river and pushed to the east. He had traveled the road to the river many times to train to cross rivers and build pontoon bridges. He traveled the Old Sayers Road to a point where the river made an abrupt turn to the west. He was headed to the site of the old Lick Switch community where the Lick Switch Ferry had once been located. The antebellum community was gone, but there were several large sand bars along the river, with easy access to the water. The Zephyr bounced down the dirt road like a shining, big, black beetle scurrying through the live oak and mesquite trees. Orvalee was further amazed by the power and suspension of the car. The dirt road was wide and well worn from the big Army trucks going to and coming from the river with loads of soldiers. Orvalee cherished the training exercises on the wide, sandy banks of the river. It was his favorite place for respite from the crowded barracks that provided little personal privacy.

He parked the Zephyr on the highest terrace above the river and walked down to the shimmering white sandbank formed along the waterside. The sandbank was rutted and disturbed from all of the training activity, but it provided a quiet beach where he could sit, relax, and think. He looked up and down the river and saw no one was around. The deep green river was flowing quietly and quickly to the south. He thought it smelled like the chicken noodle soup that was served at the mess hall. He hoped he would have some time on the river before the MPs came down the dirt road to arrest him. He smiled to himself when he thought about the major's car being reported missing. He guessed the camp MPs, Bastrop police, and Austin MPs would be swarming all over the region looking for the Zephyr. How could they miss it? He opened the telegram and read it again and continued to look at it to make sure it was real. It contained only a few words, but it sent the most important message of his life. The message hammered his brain and jabbed the pit of his stomach. She was gone. He was alone and didn't know anyone else in the world. He folded the telegram and put it in his pocket.

Orvalee sat on the sandbank and tried to figure out what he was going to do now. He had stolen a car, so he knew he would spend some time in the stockade. Shit, he thought, it was more comfortable than most of the places where he had slept in Deep Elm. He struggled with many questions.

*Who am I? Why am I here? What am I supposed to be doing with my life? What difference does it make whether I'm dead or alive? How will I die? Why am I so different from others?*

He knew he didn't have enough formal education to provide the answers, but these questions kept swirling around in his mind. He also knew he wasn't like the other soldiers in the company. They didn't come from or grow up in skid row, shanty town, hell's half acre, or Deep Elm. Most didn't know these places existed and if they did know, they surely had never visited one of them. The attitude that impressed Orvalee the most was that they didn't consider, or even believe, they could die. The Army training was serious, sober, and specific about learning to kill other people, but they joked about killing "Krauts" and "Old Mr. Hitler." They talked about their wives and girlfriends back at home. Most had pictures of women. The men that didn't have a girl in their lives had pinup pictures in their footlockers. Other than his encounter with "Putter," Orvalee never had a girlfriend, wife, or casual female friend. Orvalee was very sober and realistic about the prospect of killing another person. The other soldiers seemed to be happy-go- lucky. Most of them just wanted to have a good time in Austin. A more important motivation for Orvalee was driven by his aversion to the complex racial tensions in the barracks. Tension had been building and surfacing since the men arrived at the camp. The tension arose from the living arrangement of inductees from the northern part of the country living with inductees from the southern part of the country. Some fights had occurred in the barracks along with a daily barrage of cursing and yelling. Radio was tired of and confused by all of the friction. The officers all over the camp were busy, day and night, keeping the trainees from killing each other. The heat, newly trained aggressive behavior, close living arrangements, and racial conflict provided a volatile mix that led to verbal and physical fights.

Like Radio, the southern soldiers were used to and comfortable with referring to black people, and white people they didn't like or had trouble with, as "niggers." In fact, the racially derogatory label was deeply woven onto the language of the southern culture. Black people lived in "nigger town." Black people went to the Texas State Fair on "nigger day." And, if you put too much of a shared cigarette in your mouth, you could be accused of "nigger lippin" the cigarette. The uses of the word were pervasive, vast, deeply ingrained, and widely accepted across the southern part of the country, including Dallas and Deep Elm. The morbidity of the racial slur was increased by the use, by some white people, of much more disgusting words to refer to black people. They commonly used the derogations of "jig-a-boo," "jungle bunny," "spooks," "coons," "links," "jigs," "blue gums," and "nigs." Radio had heard all of these words in Deep Elm. In fact, he had been called a lot of unkind things while he was growing up there. He had been called "tumbleturd," "sewer rat," "rat face," "outhouse rat," "idiot," and "incubum." He didn't think anybody knew his real name. Furthermore, he didn't think about the nicknames very much, because most of the other people he knew in Deep Elm also had derogatory nicknames.

Now, the traditional racial status quo was being challenged at Camp Swift as a by-product of a culturally and regionally mixed living arrangement. On the other hand, most of the inductees from the northern part of the country were offended by the use of the racial slur. When the inductees from the south realized this, they increased the use, which escalated an already volatile group conflict. Offended soldiers from the north were now being called "nigger lovers." In addition, the black soldiers who played in a band at the Camp Swift Service Club were resented by the MPs, local citizens, and soldiers from the south. Most of the officers were hoping that the division would be shipped out before serious trouble occurred.

On a personal level, Orvalee didn't like living in the barracks. He particularly didn't like showering nude with other men or all of the horseplay that happened in the bathroom and showers. Other men would pop unsuspecting bathers with a wet towel or throw bars of soap at each other. The men regularly plotted to grab someone nude and throw them out the door at night and not let them back in the barracks for a while. The victim would pound on the door and run around the building, yelling in the windows for someone to let him inside. The other trainees delighted in the trickery. To him, the men's antics in the showers and bathroom were endless, immature, and pointless. He just didn't understand how life could seem, to them, to be so much fun and blissful in their circumstances. Radio just wanted to get away from all people.

Orvalee knew he could die because he had come close to death on several occasions. He had seen many dead people in the alleys of Deep Elm. The other soldiers had never seen a dead person and never discussed dying. They mostly talked about what they were "gonna do after the war." Orvalee didn't do anything before the war. He didn't expect to do anything important after the war. All he was sure of was that he was alive right now and on a type of journey that didn't make much sense to him, and unless he decided to kill himself, he would have to keep trying to make sense of his life. He also knew that if he died, no one would care, miss him, or grieve. He wondered what the purpose of his life was. He remembered some of the lyrics of Blind Lemon's song "Bad Luck Blues" that he had heard many times sitting in the alley next to the Harlem Club in Deep Elm.

*I wanna go home and I ain't got no clothes.*
*Doggone my bad luck soul.*
*Mama, I can't gamble, so why don't you quit trying?*
*Doggone my bad luck soul.*
*Mmm, why don't you quit trying?*

He had listened to many street preachers and storefront missionaries. The holy men had come to Deep Elm to save the poor souls who lived there. Orvalee knew most of the residents and he didn't think they were spiritually poor, only economically poor. Occasionally, he liked what one of the preachers had to say, but most of them would preach one day and then be lying in a back alley passed out drunk. The people he knew didn't go to church, but were very spiritual in the sense that they faced death often, summoned spiritual strength daily, overcame immense obstacles to survival, and recognized the existence of God on a daily basis. At least, he had heard them use the word "God" many times in their daily conversations. Orvalee wasn't sure about God, because he hadn't seen much influence of God in the lives of the people on Deep Elm.

Most people he had known, and many he didn't know, died in the street sick, cold, poor, or addicted. Many seemed to have a strong belief in God, but for him it was an abstract idea, not connected to any reality he had experienced. Now, he wanted to think about it.

He gazed at the water flowing by in the river. The wind that came with the storm, had blown the small mesquite leaves from the surrounding trees over the surface of the water. A kaleidoscope of small yellow and green leaves covered the surface of the river. The current in the river made endless swirl patterns in the leaves with many small whirlpools stretching from where he stood to the opposite riverbank. There was endless movement made by the floating leaves traveling in all directions up and down the river. He was startled by a smacking sound on the surface of the water. River carp were feeding on the small leaves. The big scaly fish were making smacking sounds all over the river when only their lips surfaced to feed on the leaves. A leaf would disappear and all that would be left was a small swirl on the surface. The sights and sounds of the river were relaxing and peaceful. He thought Mobeety would like this place. The solitude gave him a chance to think about his life.

Orvalee realized that his life was like the leaves. Each leaf was on its own, even though it looked like they were all together. They were all trapped and floating down the river, but they weren't connected. They were alone and no longer connected since leaving the tree. He realized he was alone in his journey through life. Some leaves disappeared early in the journey. The journey, for them, was quickly over and the leaves didn't have any control over their fate or the length of the journey. Others would have a long journey down the river to the Gulf of Mexico.

He thought that people were like the leaves. When they were gone, they were just gone, nothing more. He knew many unusual, colorful, strange, and marginal people in Deep Elm. They were all unique, but when they died, they were just gone. Most didn't have proper funerals, and most were buried in the city's paupers cemetery. There wasn't any fanfare, celebration, stirrings, or funerals. Most went unnoticed in life and less noticed in death. But, to Orvalee, each was remembered as one-of-a-kind in his memory and there would never be another person like them. He was more convinced now that this is the way it would be for him. He didn't know what other people thought about these ideas or "What was the word," or what did other people think about death.

He didn't see grand plan or purpose for his life. He was in the Army now, but beyond the few minutes on the riverbank, he didn't see any reason to be alive. He didn't envision a life after the Army. All of the other men in the company got pictures, letters, packages, and visitors from home. He didn't.

After he got frustrated from thinking philosophically about the purpose of his life, he now had to return to reality and decide what to do next. He looked up on the river terrace at the beautiful Lincoln Zephyr he had stolen.

He couldn't go back yet, because he hadn't spent any time driving it. He decided to go to Austin and get a swig of whiskey. He hiked up the wide, sandy riverbank to the Zephyr. He turned to take one last look at the quiet river and the green and yellow leaves on the surface of the water. It was a quiet and peaceful place, except for the sound of cooing Grey Doves sitting in the black willow trees that overhung the river. They were waiting to drink from the river in the evening. It also reminded him how alone he was in the world and trapped in his present situation.

He drove the Zephyr away from the river and back up the dirt road, crossed the railroad tracks, and turned south on the highway to Bastrop. As he drove through the town, he again thought about the little girl at the judge's home. He was fascinated with her and had observed her out of the corner of his eye the entire evening. But, in the social setting of the dinner, he was too shy and self conscious to say anything to anybody during the evening. He made sure he wasn't seen looking at her. In fact, the situation made him very tense, almost panicky, as the girl moved around the room while the soldiers were dining. He was glad and relieved when the meal was over and he was safely heading back to the camp, but he hated that he was so socially inept.

He drove through Bastrop and headed toward Austin. Instead of staying on the Austin highway, he turned north on a farm to market road that went to Webbersville and then to Austin. He took the indirect route because he knew the MPs would be patrolling the main highway. He crossed back over the river on an old iron, one lane bridge and drove to Utley, Texas where the river was in view next to the left side of the road. He parked the Zephyr, got out of the car, sat on the riverbank, and smoked a cigarette. He sat on the riverbank for about an hour before continuing on to Austin. About halfway to Austin, he noticed that the gas gage on the Zephyr was pointing to "empty." He decided to try to make it the rest of the way. He hoped he wouldn't run out of gas and get stranded beside the road. He didn't have enough money for gas and a half pint of whiskey, so he would have to steal the gas. He knew he had to get enough gas to get back to the camp, because the officers in A Company, particularly the company commander, had sternly warned the troops that AWOL was different from desertion. They told the men that soldiers could be shot or hung for desertion. The penalty for AWOL was, usually, a period of incarceration in the stockade. With these penalties in mind, he was determined to get back to the camp the next day.

When he arrived in Austin, he found a gas station on Lamar Street and parked at a gas pump. He told the attendant to put five dollars worth of gas in the Zephyr. While the attendant was pumping the gas, the Zephyr attracted a small crowd. Private Clemmons, still in uniform, nervously waited for the attendant to shut off the pump. He quickly started the Zephyr and drove away without paying for the gas. He headed south on Lamar Street, crossed the river, turned west, and headed for Zilker Park. On the way, he stopped and bought a half pint of whiskey. He parked the Zephyr at a remote spot in the park and took nips off the whiskey at different times during the evening. He fell asleep on the roomy, soft, and upholstered back seat of the Zephyr.

The next morning, he awakened and headed back to the camp. His mother had died and been buried in Dallas, and he wasn't there for the funeral, if she had one. He hoped she had a decent burial and wasn't buried in the potter's field, or a worse place, in Dallas. He didn't have anywhere to go but back to the camp. It was his only home now. He drove the Zephyr to the front gate of the camp where he knew he would be arrested. Several MPs surrounded the coupe with guns drawn, shouting and dancing around the car. They were excited, nervous, and frantic because they were caught completely off guard. A massive manhunt was taking place looking for Private Clemmons and he was now sitting in the Zephyr at the front gate to Camp Swift. Thousands of all available soldiers at the camp, all Camp Swift MPs, Austin MPs, and all local law enforcement officers had been combing the region looking for him. The guards ordered him out of the car and put handcuffs and leg shackles on him. They pushed him to the ground and dragged him to a waiting Jeep. They made him curl up and lay down in the back of the Jeep and one of the MPs said:

"If you raise your head up, I'll shoot if off, you sorry bastard."

"Yea, we'd love to shoot you now," another MP added.

Private Clemmons was puzzled about why the MPs were so angry. Soldiers took cars and Jeeps frequently and didn't get such harsh treatment. After a couple of days in the stockade, the guilty soldiers were usually assigned to a week of latrine, KP (kitchen police) duty, or some other disgusting or dirty task. They found that the officers were very clever and creative in structuring unpleasant experiences for soldiers who broke minor rules. They drove him to the stockade, searched him, booked him in, and took him to a private cell at the far end of the row of cells. The other prisoners watched intently as Orvalee was placed in a private cell.

After Private Clemmons was placed in a cell, two MPs raced to his barracks and confiscated the contents of his footlocker. It didn't contain very much. The MPs only found his issued fatigues and an envelope containing fifty dollars. It was the money his mother had given him when he left Dallas to go to Camp Swift.

Some of the other prisoners were hung over from a night of drinking, and others were still slightly intoxicated.

"Hey, private what'id you do?" one asked.

Another asked: "Are you some kind of big shot?"

"What'id you do, kill somebody?" another asked as several started laughing.

"You must be a queer for them to put you back there," another said, and then more laughter continued.

Orvalee squatted in the back corner of the cell. He was confused and getting more frightened the longer he stayed there. He didn't sleep much that night. Guards came by every hour to check on all of the prisoners. The night was punctuated by the usual snoring, grunting, farting, and cursing sounds made by a group of drunken soldiers in a jail cell. Somewhere in a back room of the stockade, a rat made the sounds of a paper sack being pushed around and torn as the animal tried to get to the contents.

Orvalee and the rest of the prisoners in the stockade were awakened by a civilian construction crew dragging and rolling welding equipment down the main hall at six o'clock in the morning. They also brought steel angle iron and steel concrete reinforcing rods down the hallway. The noise and commotion in the hallway awakened all of the prisoners who began to press their faces up to the hog wire to get a better look at what was causing all of the commotion. All of the workers, equipment, and materials were positioned in front of the last cell on the opposite side of the hallway from the cell that Orvalee occupied. They immediately started the welding machine, lit the cutting torches, and began construction of a steel reinforced cell. All of the guards and prisoners were startled, dumbfounded, and frightened by all of the activity in a place where the most activity and commotion had previously been the loud cursing from a drunken soldier.

The crew worked most of the day constructing a steel cell in place of the hog wire and wood two-by-four original cell. Smoke filled the stockade when the sparks began flashing from welders and torches that cut the steel bars in measured lengths. At one point, the welding activities set the wood floor of the stockade on fire, and construction had to be suspended briefly while the civilian crew and MPs extinguished the fire. The smoke was so thick at one point that Orvalee couldn't see the other side of the hallway. He was coughing and the other prisoners were cursing.

The new cell was completed by the end of the day. The civilian contractors took all of the equipment back to their trucks, loaded it, and drove away. Another civilian crew came in and cleaned up the mess. Shortly after they left, MPs took Orvalee out of his cell and shoved him in the new acrid smelling steel cell. The stockade got very quiet. All of the prisoners, especially Orvalee, were stunned by the activities of the day. The other prisoners whispered among themselves.

"What the hell is going on?"

"Who is this guy?"

"What did he do?"

They asked the guards, but the guards didn't provide any information. It wasn't clear who knew details about the murder, but it is likely that they didn't know much about the crime. That situation changed quickly when the guards changed shifts and left the stockade and went out into the camp community, other shifts came on duty, and the first shift came back on duty in the stockade. Word of the murder and the suspect in custody traveled quickly with several versions and significant misinformation.

Orvalee was frozen in fear when he realized the cell had been built for him. The next day, four MPs came to his cell, took him out, and walked him in handcuffs and leg shackles to a small room at the front of the building. He sat in the room with guards at the doorway for about thirty minutes. Then two officers, a major and a lieutenant, entered the room. They were from the judge Advocate General's Office. Both had an impressive collection of ribbons and medals on the chest of their uniforms.

The major was a short, slim-built man who was slightly stoop-shouldered. He had an olive complexion, deep set eyes, high cheekbones, short black hair, and a large nose. The other officer was the largest man Private Clemmons has ever seen. He was at least six and a half feet tall, square jawed, and broad shouldered. Orvalee noticed he had airborne jump wings and a ranger patch on his uniform. His muscles bulged under his uniform.

Both officers carried, on a pistol belt, a tan leather holster with a flap covering the pistol. Each flap had "US" stamped in the leather, and even though Orvalee couldn't see the pistols because of the flap, he was sure they were there. The lieutenant stood by the doorway and the major stood directly in front of Orvalee.

The major's face did not show any expression. "Are you Private Orvalee Clemmons?"

"Yes," Orvalee answered.

"You are charged with the kidnapping, rape, and murder of Polly Sue Mason," the major declared.

"I didn't kill anybody."

The major said, "We'll be back tomorrow to obtain your confession."

The two officers turned and left the room. Guards took Orvalee back to his special cell. On the way, the hallway erupted with shouts by the other prisoners.

"Murderer, baby raper, evil son of a bitch, and killer," echoed up and down the hallway. And then one of the other prisoners yelled, "The Comanche is gonna kick your ass."

Orvalee didn't know what the other prisoners were talking about, but it must have meant the major was a full or part American Indian. He surely looked Indian to Orvalee, now that he reflected on the other prisoner's outbursts. Orvalee was correct in his conclusions about the major. The officer was a Comanche and Kiowa Indian from Western Oklahoma. He had been educated in the eastern United States. He had been an Army drill instructor and then obtained a law degree. Orvalee noticed his name tag read "Pakah." He had been sent immediately to Camp Swift from Fort Sam Houston when Orvalee was arrested.

The major's primary military experience was obtained in Washington, D.C. in 1932. He was an officer in General Douglas MacArthur's 12th Infantry Regiment from Fort Howard, Maryland that attacked 43,000 members of the Bonus Army camped in Anacostia Park. The attacking force consisted of 500 infantry troops, 500 cavalry troops, six Renault tanks, and 800 police officers. They attacked 17,000 World One veterans and their families who were protesting the government's failure to pay them the bonus they were promised in 1924, for service in World War One, that couldn't be redeemed until 1945. Most of the veterans had been out of work since the beginning of the Great Depression.

After the cavalry charged, the infantry, with fixed bayonets and gas, entered the camp, evicting veterans, families, and friends. President Hoover ordered the assault stopped. However, General MacArthur, feeling the Bonus Army was a communist attempt to overthrow the government, ignored the president and ordered a new attack. Four members of the Bonus Army were killed, and over one thousand were injured. Sixty-nine police were injured. Hoover lost in a re-election to Franklin Roosevelt. In 1936, congress overrode the president's veto and paid the veterans their bonus years earlier than originally scheduled. Now the major was interrogating Private Clemmons in a murder investigation.

The rumors of the murder of the young girl had reached into the stockade. The other prisoners were agitated, angry, and excited to be so close to the focus of the rumors. They didn't consider themselves to be criminals, so for a real criminal to be in the building, it made the otherwise boring and dreary stay, quite exciting. There was a fearful excitement in Bastrop.

Skip looked through the back window of the small apartment and saw Mrs. Van Valkenberg hurrying toward the apartment. She was drying her hands in her apron and appeared to be crying. Skip quickly opened the door when the landlady arrived. The landlady screamed and cried and cried and screamed over and over when she came through the door. Skip was shocked by the landlady's hysterics.

"What happened? What happened?"

"The nigras killed the judge's daughter," she screamed out.

"What? What? What?" Skip asked when she heard the shocking news.

"Yes, yes. They murdered her," she reaffirmed.

Both women sat on the bed and cried over the death of the little girl. She said everybody in the small town knew the family, particularly the little girl. The landlady was frightened because of the rumors circulating around the town and military camp. There were rumors that a colored soldier killed the child. Another rumor claimed that a group of local colored citizens killed her in retaliation for the recent death of the colored soldier. There was also talk of a lynching. Fortunately, there hadn't been a lynching in Bastrop since 1892 when a black man, Toby Cook was murdered by a lynch mob. Unfortunately, more recent lynchings had occurred in the region. Three social realities were clear. Almost everybody in the town, colored and white, knew the little girl, where she lived, when she came home from school, and the route she took. Second, the local white citizens were outraged and wanted justice for the terrible crime. Finally, the judge's daughter was a very innocent, but high profile victim.

The judge's daughter had failed to return home from school. She usually walked home from school, and most of the citizens of Bastrop had seen her walking home many times. The school was only two blocks from her house. No one had witnessed her abduction. Poly Mason's body was found lying out in the cold in a pasture three miles from town. She had been strangled after being kidnapped. There were rumors and suspicion she had also been raped by her abductor. Very little information was released about the case, particularly in the camp newspaper and the only local newspaper. The incident was kept on the Q.T. and because of the extreme lack of information, no one knew if any other suspects were questioned. The military didn't release any information about the case. If local citizens were questioned by the military, neither the citizens nor the military were saying anything.

As soon as Polly disappeared, MPs at Camp Swift were notified of the missing girl. Of course, they were already looking for the person who stole the Zephyr. It didn't take them long to connect the two events.

It was October and it was very cold in Bastrop when the two women stayed together trying to make sense of the tragedy. Mrs. Van Valkenberg had heard all the rumors when she had gone into the town square. Both women agreed there could be serious trouble in town, but neither knew anything about the events occurring at the camp.

Frightened, worried, and tense, Skip waited for Art to come home. He wasn't scheduled to come into town that evening, but he arrived unexpectedly. When he came into the apartment, his face was ashen gray. He looked at Skip and he knew immediately she knew about the crime. Skip started crying again and they embraced for a long time.

Finally, Skip said, "The landlady said the nigras killed the judge's daughter, the little girl I made the sock monkey for."

Art quietly and slowly went to the stove, poured himself a cup of coffee, and sat down at the kitchen table. "The hell they did. They've got the man that did it in the stockade at the camp."

"What?" Skip replied in disbelief.

"Yea, it's that gawd dammed ball washer from Dallas. I knew that son of a bitch was big trouble. He should have never been in the Army."

Art was trying to stay calm, but Skip could tell by his language that he was angry and scared.

"To make matters worse, he's in my company and he stole the major's car and went to Austin...............shit!" Art then explained the switch of the cars.

Skip sat quietly waiting to see what Art wanted to do next. He had all kinds of possibilities flying around in his head, like the possibility the girl could have been killed in their car. Or, that the man could have kidnapped and killed Skip and his son.

Or, that he could have shot a group of men when he was on the firing range. He could have also killed the company's officers.

"Well, he's not going anywhere. He's locked in a special cell in the stockade......................I don't know though. Why would he kill her and drive back to the front gate?" Art pondered rhetorically.

"I guess he was so crazy he would do anything," he suggested.

"But, I never saw him do or say anything during his training," Art countered to himself.

The whole event had overwhelmed them and didn't make sense to either one of them.

"That poor little girl...........what a waste...........what a horrible waste," Skip murmured.

"Yea, and we're right in the middle of it because there will be a big investigation."

"JAG Officers and MPs will be swarming all over the place and I'll be questioned until the cows come home," Art declared.

Art got up and started pacing around the small apartment. Skip knew he was thinking while he paced. She had seen him do it before.

"The most important thing is that we don't say anything to anybody about this, especially the landlady," Art asserted.

"She felt strongly there could be racial trouble.............that colored people were to blame and the white people in town were ready to do something about the murder," Skip added.

"Yea, all hell could break loose," Art warned and then he added:

"And, we would be in the middle of it."

Art and Skip talked about moving back to Austin, but decided, for the moment, to only keep quiet.

"We can't say anything to anybody. You stay inside and I'll bring you what you need. Let's not say anything for a long time. I just want to get out of Swift and get to the next place, because eventually I'll be shipped out of here. The sooner the better," Art outlined.

"And if a race war erupts, we'll move back to Austin," Skip suggested with a serious conviction. Art could tell she was frightened and worried. He realized she was alone with their son most of the time and in a potentially dangerous situation. The killer had struck in their neighborhood. The entire Bastrop community was pierced with fear when the judge's daughter was kidnapped. Mrs. Van Valkenburg and Skip were more terrified because the kidnapping had happened in their neighborhood and the little girl lived in the next block from them.

"Okay, maybe we won't be here much longer and won't have to make another move," Art added.

After talking with Skip about the crisis, late into the night, Art went back to the camp the next day to continue training the men in his company, minus one man. Eula Johnson didn't come to work at the big house for two weeks.

A high level emergency meeting was held in the conference room at the headquarters building. It was supposed to be held in secrecy, but the Army command cars from Fort Sam Houston, entering the front gate, quickly signaled to the entire camp that the meeting was being held. The news of the meeting spread quickly and Art soon heard about the meeting. He guessed they were trying to decide what to do with the "rat" they had caught. He guessed right.

The other men in the stockade stopped yelling and Private Clemmons could finally get to sleep about two thirty in the morning. He still didn't sleep. He was nervous, scared, and worried about making a confession. He was sure he wouldn't confess to the charges, but he was worried about what they might do to him to make him confess. Having grown up in the streets of Dallas, he knew he was tougher than most of the other men. They complained about how uncomfortable the beds in the camp were and how awful the food was. He rarely had a comfortable bed or appetizing food when he was growing up.

In the stockade, he was placed on a bread and water diet and, as a result, became very hungry as he lay awake waiting for the fearful events of the next day. The next morning, Orvalee was taken to the same interrogation room. He waited about thirty minutes and the same two officers came into the room. Orvalee was trembling and starting to get dizzy when the two officers took their positions in the room. The big one stood by the door and the smaller officer, the major, stood directly in front of Orvalee. He bent over and placed his palms on the table with his fingers spread apart. Orvalee noticed that his fingers were thin, dark, and leather-looking.

The major started screaming at the prisoner, but Orvalee didn't hear the major. The major's mouth was moving, but the little girl's voice was coming out of the major's mouth. Orvalee hadn't heard her in a long time, but she was screaming at him like she always did.

*You're an evil and wicked bastard. You killed and raped that little girl. You're going to hell after they put you in front of a firing squad.*

The major screamed the accusations at him, but he didn't hear any of the charges. The major got more agitated and began waving his arms and pointing at Orvalee. When the major paused, Orvalee only said that he stole a car and went to Austin. Orvalee's minor admission only made the major more agitated, so he rapidly fired questions at Orvalee.

"When did you grab her? How did you kill her? Where did you take her?"

Orvalee said nothing. The major's face got twisted into odd contortions as he said: "We know you killed her you miserable bastard and I want a confession out of you right now................tell us what you did."

The major pounded the desk with his fists and got his face so close to Orvalee's face that Orvalee could tell the major had recently eaten some onions.

"I stole a car," Orvalee reaffirmed.

Orvalee slumped lower in the chair as the major paced back and forth in the small room.

"We're going to get a confession out of you if we have to beat it out of you," the major threatened.

They hadn't beaten him physically, but Orvalee could feel the beating would be coming soon.

The interrogations continued for three days with the same questions. He started hearing people whispering outside his cell at night. He couldn't tell what they were saying, but he was sure they were Dallas Police officers talking about him. During the interrogations, he sometimes heard the little girl screaming at him. And, at other times, he heard the major's voice. He was getting more exhausted and nervous as the days of interrogation went by. On the third night, three guards came into his cell, late at night, and beat him with bars of soap in wool Army socks. After the guards left, he lay on the floor of the cell all night in pain all over his body. The pain was particularly intense in his hands where he tried to block the blows. His hands were swollen and puffy. For Orvalee, it was like he was back in Dallas.

On the morning of the fourth day, guards took him to the interrogation room. The major and the lieutenant returned for more interrogation. Orvalee was dragging his feet and stumbling while each guard held him upright by each arm. They placed him in the same chair and started the same questions and screaming. The little girl's voice continued to come from the major's mouth. After about thirty minutes of intense questioning, Orvalee briefly became glassy eyed and then his body became stiff, rigid, and straight as a plank in the chair so that his body slid to the floor, hitting his head on the seat of the chair before his whole body hit the floor. His arms and legs shook violently and hit the legs of the table causing it to pitch around the room. The major jumped back and screamed out:

"The son of a bitch is having a seizure..................guards............. guards.......... get in here!"

Two guards rushed in and grabbed the prisoner's legs and arms and held them down. Orvalee stopped breathing when he swallowed his tongue. One of the guards freed his tongue and after a few minutes, the seizure subsided. The major continued to curse after he retreated to the hallway outside the interrogations room. After the seizure, Orvalee was exhausted, limp, and am-nesic. The guards dragged him to his cell and left him sprawled on the floor.

Most of the long nights in the Camp Swift stockade were the same. He heard  the "midnight freight" train headed north to Temple, Waco, and Dallas, Texas. It was headed back in the direction he had come from. The train to Dallas reminded him of the song he had heard Leadbelly sing in Deep Elm, "Midnight Special," written by the singer when he was in a Texas prison. Even though Orvalee had lost some of his memory of the past after he received shock treatment in the state hospital, he seemed to be able to remember the music he had listened to in Deep Elm. These nights he par-ticularly remembered some of the lyrics and melody of Blind Lemon's song "Prison Cell Blues:"

*I'm getting tired of sleeping in this lowdown lonesome cell.*
*..................I'm about to lose my mind.*

Like other residents of Deep Elm, the musicians who performed there had spent some time in a prison or jail cell. Many wrote songs and sang songs they had heard during their incarceration experiences.

He thought many times during the long nights that he had made a big mistake leaving Deep Elm. He had been in jail in Dallas, so being locked up wasn't new to him, but his current situation was confusing and frightening. He thought about "hopping" the freight train which passed outside the camp.

He wished he was on it, and he wished cousin Mobeety would come and get him out of the stockade. He talked to Mobeety many nights and the other prisoners would yell at him, "Shut up that jabbering," or "Shut up your trap, baby killer."

After the seizure incident, the major changed his interrogation approach.

Private Orvalee Clemmons was given better and larger portions of food. He was also provided an extra blanket. In addition, the specific interrogation tactics changed. He was offered incentives to confess to the crimes the Army was sure he committed. The Army was desperate to get a confession because they didn't have any physical evidence or witnesses tying Orvalee to the horrible crime. The Army also had not foreseen or anticipated that for several days after the seizure, the prisoner lost most of his memory. He couldn't even remember his name. Fearing another seizure, he was placed in a straight jacket. He was promised a lighter sentence, a lighter security prison, a federal work farm assignment, and a visit to his mother's grave site. They told him they had a witness that would testify they saw him pick up the little girl and witnesses that saw him throw the body in the field. They also told him the girl identified him as her abductor before she died. Orvalee still did not confess to the crime. He giggled upon hearing the new information.

The JAG office was becoming increasingly impatient and frustrated with the lack of a confession from the prisoner. Local tensions were rising for a resolution to the case and racial tensions were still high in Bastrop. These local conditions and Orvalee's medical condition led the Army to decide to move him to a different location. In November of 1942, he was moved to the stockade at Fort Sam Houston in San Antonio, Texas. He was moved in a half-ton Dodge Ambulance. He was restrained with a straight jacket and leg shackles during the move.

Once at Fort Sam, as it was called, a new phase of interrogation began. Orvalee was placed in a cell and then brought to a large interrogation room. The interrogators were very businesslike and factually oriented. They went over all of the details of the day he took the Zephyr to Austin. Orvalee's story was related the same way each time. He said he drove the car to the river, drove to Austin, and drove back from Austin. He continued to assert that he drove through Bastrop and didn't drive around looking for anyone. The interrogators needed to place him driving around Bastrop as part of his story. There were no witnesses that saw him driving around Bastrop in a very identifiable car. They also couldn't explain why, if he killed the little girl, he drove up to the front gate of the camp. The very calm and straight forward questioning lasted for three grueling days. The officers went over the story time after time.

On the fourth day, the interrogation procedure drastically changed. The Army investigators were becoming increasingly frustrated and impatient with a lack of a confession from Orvalee. They still didn't have any physical evidence or eyewitnesses connecting Orvalee to the crime. So, a confession was critical and their only hope for a conviction. Furthermore, they didn't want the investigation to drag on for months and years. The country was mobilizing for war, and most of the adult men in the country would be gone soon. So, the Army wanted the public to focus on the war effort and not the court martial of a soldier who committed murder in Central Texas.

The Army decided to try to get a confession from Orvalee by using "truth drugs." Twenty years earlier, a Dallas obstetrician interviewed the prisoners in the Dallas County Jail, whose guilt seemed clearly confirmed, under the influence of scopolamine. Both prisoners denied the charges on which they were held, and both, upon trial, were found not guilty. Over the next ten years, the doctor published articles in scientific journals that led to widespread use of "truth drugs" by police departments. At the time that Orvalee was being held at Fort Sam Houston, the Army was experimenting with "truth drugs" at Fort Dix, New Jersey. The Army decided to see if a "truth drug" could help obtain a confession from Orvalee that was needed for a conviction. He was injected with scopolamine and subsequently interrogated by asking the same questions that had been repeatedly asked. The interrogation did not go well and was immediately unproductive. Orvalee became drowsy with blurred vision. His heart rate increased. He reported painful headaches. He had bizarre dreams about killing people, satan, and having his clothes ripped from his body. When he did respond, he confessed to killing people in Dallas and at Camp Swift and burying the bodies in diverse locations. All of the confession was a confabulation. Orvalee started having visual hallucinations. He screamed at satan and a small girl. He spoke directly to Mobeety. He also said Mobeety told him to kill all of the people. Eventually, he got a painfully dry mouth to the point he could no longer speak, which was counterproductive to the original goal of the "truth drug." The side effects were a distraction to the central purpose of the interrogation. Unfortunately for the Army, the physiological effects incapacitated Orvalee for the following weeks, which further delayed the goal of obtaining a confession. Consequently, use of drugs was abandoned.

After little success with "truth drugs"' they put Orvalee "on the wall." They began an interrogation technique that incorporated sleep deprivation. He was placed in a standing position against a wall and guarded around the clock. While on the wall, they would continue to question him about the crime. He could eat, drink, and go to the bathroom, but he wasn't allowed to lie down and sleep. If he started to lay down, a guard would stand him up. If he passed out, a guard would awaken him and stand him back on the wall. He had more seizures.

They put him on the wall after each one with no sleep. The sleep deprivation continued for days. Orvalee lost track of the days and nights. He became delirious and started hallucinating about the Dallas Police attempting to kill him. He quickly became incoherent and then just moved his lips.

He collapsed and tried to lie down many times, but each time a guard would stand him back against the wall. The lights were always shining brightly in the room. Each day an officer approached him face-to-face and asked him if he killed the girl and if he was ready to confess. Orvalee refused to admit anything for days and days. The little girl was screaming at him more often and her visits became a daily occurrence.

*You killed her you miserable bastard. You're evil and wicked. You deserve to die and burn in hell.*

She tormented him with the same language. Sometimes she mentioned murder. Other times she mentioned rape and kidnapping.

*Tell them you did it you monster. You're going to hell anyway. Your mother was a whore and you've got the mark of the devil on your teeth.*

After five days and nights of no sleep, the officers sat Orvalee at a table and told him he could sleep if he signed a prepared confession. The confession was typed on a single sheet of paper. It stated that, after taking the Zephyr, he drove around Bastrop for some time. He saw the judge's daughter walking home from school and offered her a ride. The confession stated that he said to her: "Come on little sister, and I'll ride you home."

It stated that he rode around Bastrop with the little girl and she eventually started screaming. It stated that he strangled her with his hands and threw her in the pasture where she was eventually found. No mention was made in the prepared statement about raping her. Orvalee signed the prepared confession without reading it. He couldn't read it in his groggy, delusional, and exhausted condition. After signing the confession, the officers left the room and Orvalee was placed back in a cell.

He slept for three days. The military had the confession they needed and an immediate court martial was ordered. Orvalee didn't remember signing the confession when he awakened

# CHAPTER 6

## DEPLOYED AND DISPATCHED

The late fall winds were blowing through ancient majestic pecan trees in Bastrop, causing them to shed their nutritious and delicious cargo. The clusters had been locked away for nine months. They were splattering all over streets, yards, and buildings. Nuts and hulls made a racket when they hit the roofs of cars and buildings. Crows and squirrels created a frenzy of activity in the streets and yards as they tried to capture their share of the bounty.

The weather was changing in Central Texas, and major changes were coming to Camp Swift. The first major change, that was briefly unnoticed, was the disappearance of Major Hill and the Zephyr. He had been transferred or deployed to a different assignment somewhere else. Some time passed before anyone noticed it, but Art had not seen him since the murder of the judge's daughter. There were rumors that the MPs had seen the Zephyr in Austin. Around the camp, everyone guessed the major had sold it in Austin before he was deployed. Art was relieved he was gone, puzzled by his immediate disappearance, and mildly anxious about getting a new executive officer.

The next change hit Art and Skip like a bombshell. The entire 95th Division was ordered deployed immediately back to Fort Sam Houston. The order came down suddenly from headquarters and caught Art, and the rest of the camp, by surprise because the division was in the middle of training. Art was further stunned when he got his orders. He was the only man in the division to not be deployed. He was ordered to stay at Camp Swift and subsequently be reassigned to Company M, 387th Infantry Battalion in the 97th Division when it arrived. He tried to find out when the 97th would arrive, but he was only told the division would arrive after the first of the year, 1943.

The good news for Art was that he was promoted to captain with the corresponding pay increase. So, Art's deployment was delayed. The news of Art's delayed deployment created anxiety that normally occurs when people are faced with an avoidance-avoidance conflict, or two choices to make that are equally painful. Art and Skip were anxious to move on with their lives and away from Camp Swift, but moving on also created anxiety. They were anxious about moving closer to the inevitability of combat. They were still stuck and safe at Camp Swift, but still uncertain about the future. Art, more than Skip, didn't like being stuck. Skip, more than Art, didn't like moving on to the next assignment.

The next major change was the beginning of austerity measures at the camp. All entertaining and social activities were suspended. The black musicians at the NCO club were transferred out of the camp. Nobody seemed to know where. They were simply gone from the camp. All social goodwill activities in the surrounding communities were suspended. Even the flowers growing around the camp were eliminated. The new division commander, who had arrived before the rest of the division, refused to have flowers planted around his quarters. Art and Skip were amused by the changes and frequently laughed about how fickle the Army could be.

At the camp, as it was with other camps, there were two classifications of troops, "cadre" and "casuals," sometimes called "transitionals." "Cadre" was the name given to the soldiers permanently assigned to the camp for administration, maintenance, construction, and transportation at the camp. "Casuals" were there for training for eventual deployment. So, there were still some soldiers at the camp who were "cadre." They were mostly assigned to headquarters for day to day operation of the camp. Art was a "casual" and he assumed he had been assigned to the 97th to clean up the mess left by the 95th and provide some leadership for the training of the 97th. He was older than most field officers, so he brought some maturity to the transition. By the middle of December, most of the 95th had been deployed. Art was, as he anticipated, assigned, in the interim, the cleanup of the barracks that had been previously occupied by the 95th. He knew they would be dirty, littered, and in disarray after the hasty departure of the 95th. The trainees had no warning of the sudden move, and they were told they couldn't take anything with them except their fatigue clothes.

It didn't take long for the specifics of what he was supposed to do, to come from headquarters. He was directed to supervise a crew of soldiers who were to clean and scrub the barracks. He was also assigned the duty of emptying and inventorying all of the footlockers and removing any that needed to be repaired. Damaged footlockers were to be trucked to the quartermaster for repair. Art was also assigned to be in charge, and responsible, for inventorying all of the sheets, pillow cases, and blankets and seeing that they were all taken to the quartermaster for cleaning and repair. This inventory included three hundred and seventy two pillow cases and three hundred and eighty four sheets that Art was charged with. Art made a list of the items on a "tally sheet" and took them to warehouse No. 7 at Camp Swift. He gave Skip a copy of all of the inventory records and receipts.

Art was also responsible for over twenty four hundred small equipment items in the kitchen in the mess hall. This included the following items that he inventoried in December of 1942:

| | |
|---|---|
| Boat, sause 13 oz. (43) | Bowls, Gen use 5 ¾" (234) |
| Bowls, sugar w/cover 17 oz. (42) | Cups, coffee unhandled (234) |
| Dishes, pickle (20) | Dishes, Veg 11 7/8" (102) |
| Plates, dinner (234) | Pots, mustard w/cover (41) |
| Saucers, coffee 7" (204) | Bottles, vinegar w/stop (20) |
| Pitcher, syrup 20 oz. (41) | Shaker, pepper (41) |
| Shaker, salt (41) | Tumbler, 10 oz (234) |
| Forks, table N,S,W, (234) | Knifes, table Grille (234) |
| Spoons, table N,S,W, (234) | Pitcher, water 5 ½ qt. (20) |
| Plater, meat, 15" (20) | Cleaver, meat, 8" (2) |
| Dippers, tin 1 qt. #56 (4) | Dippers, tin 2 qt. #55 (2) |
| Filters, coffee for stock pot (10) | Forks, meat 2 prong (2) |
| Graters, tin nutmeg 5" (1) | Griddles, cast iron 20-30" (1) |
| Knives, bonning 6" (2) | Knives, bread 10" (4) |
| Knives, butcher (8) | Knives, paring M 37 4" (5) |
| Ladels,  dia, of bowl 6" (2) | Machine hd, opp sml. (1) |
| Masher, potato pounder (1) | Measure tin lqd. ½ qt. (1) |
| Measure tin lqd. 1 qt. (1) | Opener, can mechanical table (1) |
| Pans, baking 3X12X24" (8) | Pans, cake round 1X9" (7) |
| Pans, fry 11" (3) | Pans, dish 20 qt. (13) |
| Muffin pans 12 cup (25) | Pin, rolling 3 3/4X23" (1) |
| Pots, stock alum. w/cover 10 gal.(5) | Pots, stock alum. 15 gal. (2) |
| Ring adapter for coffee filter(1) | Saw, butcher (1) |
| Scales weight ctr scp 10# (1) | Scraper dough 6" (2) |
| Sieves wood 18" (1) | Skimmers, 6X15" (5) |
| Spatulas wood 37" (1) | Spoons, basting 29" retined (6) |
| Spoons, mustard wood (41) | Steels, butcher 12" (2) |
| Turner cake lge (2) | Whips, egg 10" (1) |
| Whips, egg 12" (1) | Whips, egg 16" (1) |
| Cans, corr. galv. 32 gal. (4) | |

The inventory of the kitchen equipment proved to be a documentation nightmare, cooking equipment headache, and culinary fiasco. First, there were over two thousand items that had to be located, identified, graded for damage, and documented in triplicate. Second, the official military kitchen items were mixed with non-military kitchen items that had been scrounged by the kitchen staff from some unknown source. For example, commercial pickle dishes were mixed with official government pickle dishes. Finally, kitchen personnel had collected some strange and frequently unrecognizable items for use in the kitchen. These doodads and thingamajigs were also mixed with the kitchen equipment. Art recognized the purpose of most of the items, but some seemed to be useless gimcracks. Art told Skip that the kitchen was the biggest mess he'd ever seen. Fortunately, he had worked in a hotel kitchen while he was in college, so he had an advantage over other officers who might have had to tackle the task.

The inventory of the footlockers, sheets, pillowcases, and kitchen equipment created a need for a series of letters, between Art and the Army, that lasted from the December inventory until April, 1943. The entire inventory was moved to Fort Sam Houston, and Art was charged with shortages. He found that many items, being in a chipped and cracked condition, were left in the kitchen building # T-328. He had to verify the status of the "left behind" items or be charged for them. By April 10, 1943, B Company was finally clear of any shortages of pickle dishes, sugar bowls, and sauce boats.

Finally, he was assigned the duty of inspecting all of the bunk beds to see if any needed repair and all of the bathroom fixtures to determine if any plumbing fixtures needed repair. If anything was damaged or broken, he had to submit a written work order to headquarters. He knew there were plumbing problems in the barracks, because he had submitted work orders in the past. Nothing had been done about the leaks and malfunctions. Art guessed that if the war lasted very long, the wood floors in the bathrooms would be rotten and collapse before it was over.

For all of the items taken to the quartermaster, Art was instructed to make sure he got a receipt for them when he gave them to the quartermaster. Art knew that documentation in the transfer of items was important. He didn't want the Army billing him for anything. It was grubby and inglorious work, but he got to spend most of his time in a warm barracks and he wasn't sleeping on the ground in a tent or being shot at by an enemy soldier. Furthermore, there weren't any trainees at Camp Swift to be trained by Art. The cleaning of the barracks went as planned. Bathrooms and floors were scrubbed and disinfected. Cleaning supplies and equipment were drawn from the quartermaster.

Art inventoried all of the sheets, pillowcases, and blankets and noted, on the inventory form, the ones that needed repair. They were all trucked to the quartermaster, and Art got a receipt for the entire shipment.

The footlockers were a bigger problem. The wooden boxes, where each soldier had kept  personal items and clothes, were bulky and full of trash and debris. Many were broken or damaged. The footlockers were left from the First World War, so they were weak, splintered, or unhinged. Names had been stenciled on the boxes and removed many times. For these reasons, Art had all of the lockers, including the ones in the BOQ, brought to B Company's barracks.

The men stacked the boxes in the day room. They filled the room to the ceiling. Art started an inspection line to empty the footlockers into trash barrels. The barrels filled quickly because the footlockers contained a lot of residue and items the soldiers would have removed from the footlockers if they had received a warning of the move. The most frequent items falling into the barrels were cigarettes, matchbooks from Austin bars, used ditty bags, half pint whiskey bottles, Camp Swift postcards, pin-up pictures, C rations, moldy food, and paper goods, especially toilet paper. Art was amazed and puzzled upon seeing that soldiers would hoard toilet paper until one of the soldiers reminded him that a lot of the men came from homes where commercial toilet paper wasn't available or it was a bathroom luxury. Spoons, forks, cups, and other items from the mess hall were rescued and returned. He was amused when he found spent shell casings with holes drilled in them. The trainees wore them on a string for jewelry, souvenirs, or good luck charms. Occasionally, the work crew would erupt in laughter, whoops, and hollers when they found packs of "rubbers" or a pair of lady's cotton panties, and if they got lucky, silk ones. One of the men would hold the panties in the air, and the whole group would cheer and dance around the work site. The crew was definitely having a good time finding all of the treasures in the footlockers. In addition, they would speculate which items belonged to specific departed soldiers. Art was amused by the crew having such a good time with such a disgusting assignment. He related the story many times during and after the war.

Art's work crew was dumping the contents of the footlockers, and Art was inspecting the lockers for integrity. They had filled two barrels of trash and loaded the barrels on a truck outside the barracks. The crew picked up a footlocker and turned it up. As the trash cascaded into the third barrel, a sock monkey fell out.

"What the hell?" Art asked rhetorically.

The crew looked in the barrel, and one of the soldiers retrieved the sock monkey and handed it to Art.

"What the hell is *that* doing here?" he again asked rhetorically.

The soldiers looked at each other and shrugged their shoulders without an answer.

Art immediately recognized the stuffed monkey, so he told the men to go outside and take a cigarette break. Art then sat at a desk and tried to figure out how the sock monkey Skip had made for the judge's daughter, who was now dead, got into one of the footlockers. He looked at the locker that had held the monkey to see if there was a name on it. He didn't see one. Many names had been removed and painted over. He didn't know which building the locker came from.

"Shit! How did it get here?" Art said.

Questions raced through his mind.

*Which building did it come from? Was this Private Clemmons' footlocker? Was it somebody else's locker? How did it get from the little girl's house to the barracks? Did the little girl have it with her when she was kidnapped? Did the killer take it and then hide it in the footlocker? How was the sock monkey connected to the murder? Should he return it to her parents? Should he take it back to Skip? Should he throw it away? What tha hell is going on here? Was the killer somebody other than Private Clemmons?*

Art was stunned, bewildered, and scared. He considered whether he should tell Skip. He knew she would be shocked and scared. What he knew for sure was he didn't want to get drawn into an investigation, but the appearance of the sock monkey was a mystery. Art knew the sock monkey was in an odd, unexpected, and perplexing place.

Art threw the monkey back in the barrel and called the soldiers to come back to finish the inspection and cleaning of the footlockers. When he took the footlockers to the quartermaster, he was two short of the number on the inventory. He remembered that two soldiers had been transferred to the "Cooks and Bakers School" at Fort Sam Houston. He had to get documentation that verified they had taken the footlockers with them. The next evening, he told Skip what had happened and, while they were both sad, confused, and scared, they agreed to continue to keep everything on the Q.T. They were, now, very ready to leave Bastrop and Camp Swift.

Art obtained a ten day leave at Christmas, 1942. They celebrated Christmas in the apartment. Their son received gifts of money, a Mother Goose book, fifteen dollars in War Savings Stamps from the 379th Regiment, block toys, and electric train, a drum, a stuffed dog, and a stuffed elephant.

Rumors about Private Clemmons were circulating around Camp Swift and Bastrop like the fallen brown pecan tree leaves blowing around the streets of Bastrop. He was gone from the camp, but left in his place was wild speculation about where he was and what had happened to him. One rumor was that he had been executed by a military firing squad. Another rumor suggested he had escaped from custody and was back at Camp Swift. Some people said they had talked to other people who had talked to people who had seen him in Austin. The rumors were factually as elusive, fanciful, and mysterious as the coyotes that inhabited Camp Swift. Rumors around military bases were quite common, so Art and Skip ignored them most of the time.

Art and Skip knew the private was undergoing a court martial in San Antonio. They also knew Art could be subpoenaed to testify at the court martial. They didn't like that possibility.

Art didn't know about anybody who had been subpoenaed, but the camp headquarters had become very quiet, and no information had come out about the court martial. Art accidently met and talked to an executive officer on the walkway to the camp headquarters. He said that the unofficial word about the situation was that everyone was supposed to not say anything to anybody about anything associated with the case. Art told Skip that everybody was tight-lipped, but the rumors continued.

Art didn't think anybody in the Army knew that he knew Private Clemmons in Dallas before war was declared, and they both were sent to Camp Swift. But, Art knew that the private could tell them that he knew Art before the war, especially under interrogation. So, with the tension in the area about the murder, the possibility of a subpoena, and the opportunity for a relaxing trip, they decided to take a long trip. A trip to the north, west, or east could put them in inclement weather, so they decided to head south.

The day after Christmas, the family left for a trip to Monterrey and Saltillo, Mexico in the Dodge. They drove through San Antonio and headed for the Mexican border. During the trip, Art and Skip celebrated their fourth wedding anniversary.

When they returned to Bastrop, there was still a lot of tension and anger in the community and the potential for violence. The accused killer of the judge's daughter was in custody, and most people were relieved. Still, a few other people were apprehensive that the man in custody might not be the killer. The deep current of fear that ran through the entire community was based on the suspicion that a black person had killed her. That was the initial reaction when word of the crime first went out to the public. Some of the suspicion was now mixed with a wary confusion.

On the 19th of January, a strong cold front blew through the area, and the temperature quickly dropped to serious levels. On the second night of the cold snap, the temperature went down to eleven degrees. The camp wasn't prepared for the severe freeze and as a result, the motor block in Art's Jeep along with three hundred motor blocks froze and cracked. None had been drained before the freeze. All of the vehicles were inoperable until the blocks were replaced. Art and Skip were worried that the Army was going to charge the officers responsible for the vehicles for replacing the damaged blocks. All of the blocks had to be replaced, so an extensive repair program was started. A survey was made of the damaged vehicles and, to Art and Skip's relief, the damaged vehicles were erased from the records of the responsible officers. Along with Skip's birthday, they celebrated the good news on January 24th.

All of the 97th Division had arrived at Camp Swift by February 1, 1943. The training for the 97th was more strenuous than it had been for the 95th Division. The new division commander took hikes with his troops. Many times on Sundays, he would be seen hiking alone in the training area, timing himself, so that he would know what to expect from his men and to see whether they were getting trained under rugged conditions.

Private Orvalee Clemmons was ordered to have a court martial. His confession was the primary evidence that convicted him. Prior to conviction, he was examined by three psychiatrists to determine if he should stand trial. The first two Army doctors spent very little time with Orvalee. They asked him a few questions about whether he knew he committed a crime and whether he thought it was wrong to do it.

The third doctor spent several hours with Orvalee over several sessions. His name was Dr. Elias Rosenbaum. Dr. Rosenbaum told Orvalee that he was from New York City, but the doctor didn't reveal anything else about himself. He asked a lot of questions and was very patient and understanding with Orvalee. Dr. Rosenbaum questioned Orvalee while he was lying on an Army cot that had been placed in his office.

During the first group of one hour sessions, the doctor asked about early childhood diseases, head injuries, painful headaches, and treatment in the state hospital. The doctor took a lot of notes while Orvalee answered the questions. Other than the time in the state hospital, Orvalee had never seen a doctor for any kind of disease or injury. Orvalee explained that he had suffered from seizures as long as he could remember. The doctor's questions in the second group of sessions became more intrusive about Orvalee's life. He asked him about previous ECT, drug use, and alcohol use. He asked him if he heard voices, noises, or buzzing sounds in his head. Orvalee answered that he had heard people whispering about him many times. He also said a little girl talked and sometimes screamed at him. He inquired if he had experienced unusual smells and if people or objects had intense odors. Orvalee replied that he thought that objects had strong or unusual smells.

He asked him if he had ever tried to, thought about, or planned to kill himself or another person. Orvalee said he couldn't be sure, because the memory of his past experiences was now mixed with his past bad dreams and recent fantasies. He told the doctor that he had thought about killing his mother, but he didn't know why. He said he had dreamed about being lynched by a mob, but the faces in the mob were gone or just blank spaces. He had also dreamed about being buried alive under a pile of manure. All of his dreams were violent. Later he remembered a dream he had many times.

In the dream, he was riding in a shiny black coupe traveling backward over a cliff.

The doctor listened intently and wrote down much of what Orvalee related. Sometime Orvalee would answer with little emotion or nonverbal expression, like he was stone faced. Other times he would grimace, wince, and giggle during his answers. The doctor asked again if he had ever planned, thought about, or tried to kill himself. Orvalee quickly answered that he had thought about it at one time in his past. He had become very blue and down-hearted after a Dallas Police Officer did something very bad to him when he was twelve years old. The doctor didn't say anything or probe and let Orvalee take his time. Nothing was said for about ten minutes. Orvalee finally related how a police officer made him get in his police car. The officer drove to a deserted back alley and forced Orvalee to give him a blowjob. The officer then kicked him out of the car and drove away, but not before he told Orvalee he would kill him if Orvalee told anybody what had happened. Orvalee believed the threat and never told anybody, until now. After the incident, he had thought about killing himself by jumping off the Houston Street Viaduct. Orvalee saw the officer on two later occasions. On each occasion, the officer pointed his service revolver at him. The officer must have left Dallas, because Orvalee never saw him again.

The doctor then asked him if he had ever thought about killing young girls. Orvalee grimaced.

He then blurted out, "I hate 'em."

The doctor didn't respond.

"They sneak into my mind and won't leave," Orvalee added.

He went on, "But, I'm so attracted to them. I hate 'em. I hate me for wanting 'em."

Orvalee's body became rigid, he clenched his fists, and formed a fetal position on the cot with his body. His eyes flashed up and down, right and left. He appeared to the doctor to be in a state of terror. The doctor remained silent. With his body tied up like a knot, the prisoner let out a loud and unrecognizable scream, "Moooobeeeetiiii."

The doctor blinked and then heard the MP's moving around on the other side of the door. They had been quietly guarding the interrogation room when they heard the scream. The doctor could tell Orvalee was in the middle of a psychotic episode and suffering from internal conflict and chaos.

When Orvalee's spell seemed to subside, he told the doctor that a twelve year old girl had talked to him many times. The doctor asked him if she had talked to him during the interview. Orvalee replied that she had, but her voice was far away, faint, and imperceptible. He said it was like someone hearing the voice of a person far off in the river bottoms when the listener was on a high bridge.

"What does she usually say to you?" the doctor asked.

"She says I'm wicked and evil," Orvalee replied.

"She says I'm possessed by the devil," Orvalee added.

"And what does she say about your present situation?" the doctor probed.

"She says I killed the judge's daughter," Orvalee added.

"And?" the doctor asked and then waited for him to continue.

"She says I killed her, but I didn't. I was angry and scared when I saw her in her home, but I didn't kill her," Orvalee insisted. "And I didn't rape her either. I was so angry that when I got back to the barracks, I hurt my hand smashing the wall in the shower room."

"Go on."

"They made me sign that confession when I was tired and exhausted," he insisted. "I didn't read it and I don't know what it said."

"How do you feel about that?"

"I don't know. I'm so confused and I don't know what I've done………….. the little girl that screams at me said I did it. She says I'm evil."

Orvalee started giggling.

He ended the final session, in this group of sessions, with a question about whether he had experienced violent dreams. Orvalee replied that he had experienced violent dreams many times.

"What about violent fantasies?" the doctor asked.

"Yea, I've had lots of 'em," Orvalee replied.

"When do they happen?"

"When I get nervous or under a lot of pressure, especially when I'm around young women," Orvalee explained.

"What about violent dreams?"

"Yea, I have them also. It is usually something bad happening to me."

"Tell me about one," the doctor said.

"Well, the one that happens over and over is the one where I'm set on fire and hung from a bridge, light pole, or tree." Orvalee paused. "I don't die though. I just hang there and suffer in pain. It's terrible, but I dream about it."

"How often do you have this dream?"

"Sometimes only once a month, but it happens at least every three months. The surroundings change, but it is the same." The prisoner paused and then very quietly speculated, "I guess I'm pretty crazy, huh?"

The doctor didn't respond, but he knew Orvalee had become more comfortable talking to him. He had to be careful about going into too much depth with Orvalee, even though he was trained to do so. He was in a position only to determine Orvalee's competence to stand court martial. He was trained to treat Orvalee's condition, therefore he was intellectually and professionally drawn to the complexities of Orvalee. He would have, in other cases with a patient, been professionally responsible for getting at the underlying causes of Orvalee's problems and trying to cure him of his mental disorders. He had been trained to work with patients like Orvalee and had been successful with many patients, even though he was considered new to the profession and a young professional doctor. Nevertheless, he was charged with only determining the prisoner's level of sanity or insanity.

In the final group of sessions, the doctor asked Orvalee about sexual fantasies. Orvalee said he had them many times.

"When do they occur?" the doctor asked.

"When I think about women and when I get angry and panicky around them," Orvalee explained. "I want sex with women, but I can't have 'em. They invade my brain and won't go away. I try to get 'em out, but they come back, again and again."

"And that makes you angry and desperate."

"Yea, really angry, but it scares me that I might not be able to control myself."

"Have you ever been unable to control yourself?" the doctor asked.

"Yea, many times. I blow up and smash things."

"How often do these fantasies occur?"

"All the time, too many times to count."

"Do they always involve sex?"

"Sometimes yes, but sometimes no."

"And with sexual dreams?"

"Oh yea, always with dreams."

"So you feel helpless, possessed, and trapped by these dreams," the doctor said.

Orvalee waited a long time to respond to the doctor's statement. Finally he mumbled under his breath, "Mobe.........Mobe..........Mobe......... Mobe." He then began to giggle and cover his face with his hands.

The session slowed because of long periods of silence between the two men. The doctor asked him about his relationship with his mother and father. Of course, Orvalee didn't know about his father, because he didn't know who his father was. The doctor again asked Orvalee about whether he hated his mother.

"Sometimes I did. But, most of the time she was my only friend and relative. I loved her very much, but she's dead now." Orvalee paused for several minutes "When I heard she had died, I took the Lincoln to Austin. The news came and I panicked."

Orvalee cried a lot during the final group of sessions. He had never talked to anyone about the subjects the doctor brought up in the sessions. The subjects in the final group of sessions were very painful to discuss with the doctor, and Orvalee was exhausted, but relieved when they were over. He was also relieved that he wasn't the only person that knew his deeply painful secrets. That night he dreamed about being in the shiny black car going over a cliff. It was similar to past dreams, but in this dream, the car was almost to the point of crashing in the bottom of an abyss.

The doctors were not in agreement on the issue of his mental competence. His record clearly indicated he had spent time in a Texas mental hospital. Two of the doctors were in favor of his standing trial, but one was not. Dr. Rosenbaum, the dissenting doctor, made several points in his reports and testimony.

First, he reported that Orvalee had suffered from epileptic seizures since he was a child. The frequency and severity of the seizures had increased as he had gotten older and had increased while he was in custody.

Second, Orvalee had a history of mental illness and had been hospitalized for a serious disturbance. Furthermore, the Army knew his record when he was admitted for service in the Army.

Third, Orvalee suffered from delusions and hallucinations which severely affected his contact with reality, his ability to know right from wrong, and his ability to provide a coherent interview or confession. He was diagnosed as a Hebephrenic Schizophrenic and was suffering delusions of sin and guilt, persecution, and demonic possession. He suffered from auditory hallucinations of people whispering about him, a small girl screaming at him, imaginary friends and relatives talking to him, and dreams when he was awake. The voices were "command hallucinations" telling him he committed the crime. Sometimes the little girls told him what to do and at other times, and imaginary friend or relative told him what to do. As far as the doctor could tell, these symptoms had persisted since the prisoner (he had to be careful not to use the term "patient") was an adolescent.

Fourth, the doctor reported that Orvalee was suffering from extreme emotional disintegration. He responded inappropriately to emotional cues. He giggled and laughed when he would be expected to be emotionally serious, and he got angry when he would be expected to be emotionally happy.

Fifth, he testified that psychotic patients frequently make "conscience-tricken" confessions to crimes they did not commit. In this case he confessed under command of a voice in his head.

Sixth, the doctor reported that the prisoner's condition was rapidly deteriorating.

Finally, the doctor concluded Orvalee was clearly psychotic and not competent to stand trial, based on Orvalee's hospital records and the clinical interviews conducted while Orvalee was in custody. The doctor was outvoted two to one. Therefore, Private Clemmons was declared not insane and thus competent to stand trial.

After a military court martial, Private Orvalee Clemmons was found guilty and sentenced to hang with no appeal. Orvalee was a soldier, so a final decision to carry out the sentence had to come from President Franklin Roosevelt, Commander-in-Chief of the Armed Forces. A telegram was sent to Judge Mason that read:

"Confidentially, matter is ending to your satisfaction."

The telegram came from Washington, D. C., but it didn't indicate who sent it; therefore, it wasn't signed.

Private Orvalee Clemmons was held in the stockade in solitary confinement at Fort Sam Houston until the sentence was to be carried out. The Mason family was notified that the execution would take place at Leon Springs Military Reservation.

The site was twenty miles outside San Antonio. Two platforms were constructed about seventy five feet apart. One was for viewing the execution; the other was the gallows, which was level with the viewing platform. The two elevated platforms stood in stark contrast to the surrounding hill country foliage. They looked like large yellow pine scaffolds that should more appropriately be supporting elevated gas or water tanks like Private Clemmons had seen at Camp Swift. He grimaced when he smelled a strong odor of chlorine coming from the boards. Also, someone had hastily splashed the word "justice" in olive drab paint on the fascia boards of the platform.

When Orvalee arrived at the execution site, he was shocked and confused by the lack of people in attendance. He expected there would be a large, screaming crowd like he had seen at the hanging in Dallas when he was a child. Not very many people wanted to see him die, but he still wondered if people would cut his clothes off his body for souvenirs. There were a few newspaper reporters at the execution. Their cars, two Army command cars, and an Army ambulance were parked on the dirt road at the execution site.

On March 19, 1943, Orvalee Clemmons climbed the traditional thirteen steps to the top of the gallows platform. He was in uniform, but the brass military buttons had been replaced by plain civilian buttons. As he climbed the steps, he remembered some of the lyrics of Blind Lemon's song, "See that my grave is kept clean."

*Well, there's one kind of favor I'll ask you.*
*You can see that my grave is kept clean.*
*Well my heart stopped beating and my hands turned cold.*
*Now I believe what the Bible told.*
*Did you ever hear that coffin' sound?*
*Means another poor boy underground.*

Two MPs assisted Private Clemmons in getting out of the Army ambulance that had been converted to a paddy wagon. He was bound by handcuffs and leg irons. Two more MPs watched in ready to help the first MPs, in case the condemned man became violent. Private Clemmons shuffled to the first step of the gallows and stepped on the first step. He started giggling and acting silly. He shook his legs like wet spaghetti and continued the unusual antics until he reached the seventh step. The MPs were cursing. Two were on each side of the condemned man and two were three steps lower with their arms extended, pushing Private Clemmons from behind.

When the group reached the seventh step, Private Clemmons suddenly pitched backwards into the air. His feet were still on the seventh step, but his head was now near the first step. His eyes rolled back, and his arms and legs shook violently as much as the restraints would allow. The MPs were shouting, grunting, and cursing. They grabbed him and tried to get him upright. The chains on the leg irons were slapping against the wooden stairs. Other MPs rushed to assist the group so that the scene looked like a vertical rugby scrum. Private Clemmon's face turned blue after he swallowed his tongue. When the group finally got him to the top, one of the MPs who was also a medic, cleared his airway. After a lot of cursing, the execution proceeded.

When Orvalee got to the top of the gallows, he recovered and looked over the tops of the mesquite and mountain cedar trees. The bright green leaves of the mesquite trees stretched for miles. It was a view he loved, but he knew it was soon to be his final moment to view the beauty. He remembered the leaves of the river and how many disappeared on their journey down the river. Like the leaves, he was about to disappear.

*You wicked bastard. You raped and killed that little girl. You're going to die for it. It's your punishment for being an evil and crazy fiend. Ha! Ha! Ha!*

He looked up at the overcast sky, and as the drizzle hit his face, he yelled, "Ma! Ma! They're going to kill me!"

His voice broke the misty silence of the execution site. The drizzle not only wet the entire scene, but also muffled his outcry, as if the wet mesquite and mountain cedar trees soaked up the sound of his voice. Except for the trunks of the mesquite trees that had turned from their normal gray to black from the rain, Orvalee noticed how familiar the scene was. It reminded him of his time on the Colorado River.

He looked away from the small group and saw an elderly man standing under the mesquite and mountain cedar trees. He was wearing white painter's overalls turned inside out so that all of the paint on them couldn't be seen, except for the dark colors that had soaked through to the other side of the cloth. He wore the top of a pair of red long johns with the sleeves cut off as a shirt, under the overalls. It was Mobeety. Orvalee was sure it was him.

He blinked his eyes and the man was still there. He silently formed the words with his mouth, "Uncle Mobe."

He smiled because he was surprised and pleased that a family member would come to his execution. Now, all of his family and friends on Deep Elm would know what happened to him. And, he wouldn't die alone because Mobeety Munson was there with him.

They put the noose around his neck and he noticed that it was the same kind of olive drab rope he had used to pull boats and pontoon bridge sections on the river. They were using an official Army rope. Then, the rope had burned, bloodied, and cut his hands, and now it was going to do the same to his neck.

The guards were startled at his previous outburst and quickly indicated that the trapdoor was ready to be sprung. The trapdoor was sprung, his body dropped down, and the hard coarse noose tightened around his neck. Before his blood and oxygen were completely cut off from his brain, he saw a brilliant white light and then he saw himself being swallowed by an enormous river carp. Then he ceased to exist. Orvalee Clemmons, who had been known as "Radio" for most of his life, was dispatched from this earth on March 19, 1943, five months after the commission of the crime for which he was convicted. He was the fifth of one hundred and forty-one prisoners executed during World War II.

Orvalee's body was lowered to the ground. The noose was removed, and he was pronounced dead by an Army doctor. His body was covered with an oil soaked Army truck tarp. The water dripping from the gallows hit the rigid canvas tarp and made a sound like marbles bouncing on a table top. There was not a family member present to view his execution, no one to claim or bury his body, and no one to notify of his death. The Army shipped his body to Dallas accompanied by a dark brown leather documents pouch containing his military records and an envelope holding the fifty dollars his mother had given him when he left Dallas to go to Camp Swift. His body passed Camp Swift on the "midnight freight" train headed to Dallas. Like it did every night, the train whistle blew as the train passed the camp. The men in the stockade heard the whistle, but they were unaware of the fact that the train was carrying the body of the camp's most notorious and infamous resident in the history of the camp and one of the few soldiers executed during World War Two. He was buried in the Dallas City Paupers Cemetery. The cemetery is now under a church. One representative for the Mason family had stood on the top of the viewing platform and viewed the execution.

Except for regional newspaper articles, there was virtually no media coverage of the trial and execution, and the camp and city knew very little about the events. Art and Skip returned to the routine of training the troops.

After March, news of the execution began to slowly drift into Bastrop and the Camp until most of the people in the area knew what happened to the soldier who was executed for the crime. Art and Skip were relieved when he was taken to Fort Sam Houston and more relieved that the terrible event was over. Art and Skip had spent many nights discussing the events, late into the night. They had many unanswered questions about the murder of the judge's daughter. Art was bewildered by the fact that the Army hadn't interviewed him or anybody else at the camp that he knew about. There were a lot of soldiers close to Private Clemmons that knew him and Art had known him before the war. The Army didn't know that Art had known him, before the war, but had they asked, he would have told them what he knew about the man. They wondered if the Army had the right man. They wondered how all of the pieces fit together, the sock monkey, Major Hill, the killing of the black soldier, and Private Clemmons. They knew that they may never hear the true story. They were right about that part of the mystery. The story was over as far as the Army was concerned. New and unaware troops arrived at Camp Swift. It seemed hopeless to Art and Skip to discuss it any more. They had endured sporadic fear, looming dread, chronic apprehension, and many sleepless nights on top of the day-to-day stress of training troops for war mobilization. They were like the rest of the community that wanted the concern about the murder to blow away with the zephyrs from the east that stroked the Lost Pines of Bastrop State Park and fanned the dusty fields of Camp Swift. But, the late night discussions began a tradition between them that would last the rest of their lives. They never mentioned the event again.

There was still an uneasy atmosphere in Bastrop for years, but local citizens did not openly discuss the events. Ostensibly, they wanted to respect the privacy of the Judge's family and heal the wounds of the crime and reduce racial tensions. All of the soldiers were eventually deployed—many were killed or wounded in the war. But a deep undercurrent of distrust and suspicion persisted for years after the camp was abandoned and disassembled. In November of 1943, Art was deployed to Fort Polk, Louisiana with the 97th Division. Before leaving the little white house on Water Street, the family took pictures in front of the house. Art loaded their few belongings in the Dodge and drove them to Louisiana. For Skip, who was pregnant, they weren't leaving Bastrop soon enough.

The training conditions at Fort Polk were much worse for Art than they had been at Camp Swift, because Art and the 97th Division became a part of the environmentally miserable and notorious Louisiana Maneuvers that involved half a million soldiers, and took place on over 3,400 square miles. The maneuvers gave the Army a chance to test a new doctrine that stressed the need for a massive number of troops to be mobile and move long distances in combat.

For Art, it meant weeks in the field commanding a company of men and moving them from one objective to another in miserable conditions. In January and February of 1944, the temperature dropped. It snowed and drizzled over the entire maneuver area. The troops were cold and wet. The only way to stay warm was to burn pine tree stumps, which were rich with highly flammable pine pitch. They would burn when everything else was wet and wouldn't burn. Unfortunately, the burning stumps emitted black smoke and soot that covered the troops. who were trying to stay warm. Art couldn't stand the filth, soot, and acrid odor that had covered him, so he decided to leave without permission (AWOL) to go home to Skip, to take a bath, and to get a clean uniform. Skip told the story many years later.

While at Fort Polk, they had another son. Art was subsequently deployed to Fort Leonard Wood, Missouri and then to England to prepare for the invasion of Europe. In March of 1944, Art received the following items that had been shipped from Fort Meade, Maryland:

1  Carbine, cal. .30 M1
1  Oiler, carbine, cal. .30 M1
1  sling, carbine, cal. .30 M1
7  magazines, assy. for carbine M1
1  pouch, waterproof, carbine M1
1  thong
1  brush, thong
3  brush, cleaning.

He now had his own equipment for fighting in the war in Europe.

Art and Skip drove the Dodge to New York after leaving the boys in Iowa with Skip's parents. Before Art boarded a ship bound or England, they saw a Broadway play. In England, he was assigned to the 29th Division.

While he was in England, he received a bill for fifteen hundred dollars for the sheets and pillow cases at Camp Swift that the Army asserted he had failed to return to the quartermaster. Art and Skip were furious. It took extensive paperwork and correspondence with the Army before the matter was cleared. He didn't have to pay for the items. Fortunately, Skip had a record and receipt for the items.

Before returning to Dallas after the war, Art was sent to Kennedy General Hospital in Memphis, Tennessee. Kennedy General Hospital was a central facility in the Army's "Reconditioning Program" through which convalescing patients were treated and reconditioned for return to duty through planned exercises and athletics and by the constructive use of leisure time in educational pursuits. When Art arrived, the hospital was very crowded. In the three years the hospital was in operation, it cared for over 44,000 patients, so it was understandable that Art would find the hospital so crowded.

The hospital specialized in orthopedic surgery, thoracic surgery, neurology, and psychiatry. Art was treated for symptoms related to combat fatigue which included crying spells, hypervigilance, depression, anger, and hysterical conversion reaction.

Conversion reaction was a type of psychoneurosis that frequently included symptoms of numbness in the hands, paralysis of the hands, and intense sweating of the palms of the hands. Art had experienced paralysis of the hands along with other psychoneurotic symptoms. The following document was Art's official medical record:

Brief Clinical Abstract

Captain Arthur Leo Shafer

Brief medical history of the case: This 32-year old Captain, Infantry, with 3 ½ years of service, entered Brooke General Hospital on 29 May 1945 as an evacuee from the ETO via Kennedy General Hospital.

Past history reveals a very nervous child who was easily excitable and chewed his finger nails. He managed to complete college at the age of about 25, having worked his way to a large degree through school. His family history revealed considerable friction amongst his parents and an extremely nervous and neurotic mother. Patient entered the Army as a 1st lt. in March 1942 and entered combat in France on D-Day plus 5. He remained in combat until the 12 July as a company commander, when he was evacuated out for a flesh wound of the right hip. While he was in the hospital it was noted that he had a great deal of anxiety. An attempt was made to return to duty, but on his first engagement he found himself in a dangerous position and became hysterical, broke out crying, and complained his hands were paralyzed. He then became unable to talk. He was evacuated through channels to Kennedy General Hospital where, after receiving treatment, he was transferred to the Convalescent Hospital at this center. It was felt that he was unsuitable for conservative therapy and he was transferred to a general hospital ward.

In the hospital here the patient's chief symptoms were marked by depression, constant anxiety, and "crying jags." He was continually nervous and apprehensive. He was sent on sick leave and showed only a very slight superficial improvement. His sleep cycle was slightly disturbed in that he could not go to sleep until the early morning hours. Examinations through the various hospitals revealed no evidence of any organic pathology. These examinations, including an EEG were normal. After many months of hospitalization, the anxiety state was very little better than at the time he was admitted to the hospital.

Art was treated inpatient, for six months, for combat fatigue. One of the treatment procedures was crafts. He made leather purses and scarves for Skip. The scarves were made from surplus, recycled silk parachutes. The other treatment was ECT. He was placed in a straight jacket and administered ECT. He also made a pair of stilts in wood crafts therapy for his eldest son.

After six months, he was released from the hospital in Memphis. After he was released, Art, Skip, and the two boys moved back to Dallas. Art continued to play golf at Bob-O-Links golf course with Bill Buchan. The difference now was that golf was part of an outpatient treatment program. The doctors in Memphis told him to participate in activities where he hit something. Golf and tennis were recommended. So, his golf at Bob-O-Links had a different purpose than it did before the war. Some of the doctors in Memphis were very pessimistic about his chances for recovery. Golf, tennis, and outer outdoor activities must have been effective. He had few occurrences of any manifest symptoms of combat fatigue in later years except for mysterious chronic itching in his hands. Only Skip knew if there were any covert symptoms.

What did last, on a higher plane of honor and accomplishment, were the commendations Art received for service in Normandy and the Rhineland. These awards far overrode, overshadowed, and outlasted any medical concerns after the war,

He returned with a Purple Heart Medal for being wounded in combat. He also received the French *Medaille Du Jubile* for serving in Normandy, France. Finally, he returned with a Silver Star Medal. The citation from the Headquarters of the 29th Infantry Division, Commanding General, for the Silver Star read:

> "For gallantry in action against the enemy in Normandy, France. On 17 June 1944, after his company had made a short withdraw in order to set up a defensive position, Captain Shafer discovered that three wounded men had been left at the forward area. Taking three volunteers with him, Captain Shafer made his way under intensely heavy machine gun and sniper fire to the men and carried them back to the limits of the company. By his prompt action, the lives of the men were saved. The cool courage and high regard for his men displayed by Captain Shafer reflect great credit upon himself and the Military Service. Entered Military Service from Iowa."

The citation was signed by C.H. Gerhardt, Major General, U.S. Army, Commanding.

In the early 1950s, most of Deep Elm was torn down to make way for the city's first freeway, Central Expressway. In 1956, the railroad tracks were removed to provide right of way for Central Expressway. Like the memories of Deep Elm, the stories of the elusive, mysterious, and mythical Mobeety Munson faded away in Dallas. His legacy was a few lines sung or recited by schoolchildren for several years.

> Old Mobeety walked the streets of Ellum Deep.
> Searching for lost and tortured souls to reap.
> Some people say he was just a man; others say a ghost from hell.
> So mammas hide your children well.
> 'Cause old Beety will snatch 'em while they sleep.

In 1958, fifteen years after Art, Skip, and their son lived in Bastrop and the year Art's oldest son graduated from high school, an un-disseminated, unofficial, un-publicized, and sole history of Camp Swift was written by two high ranking individuals who played a major role in the development of the camp. At the time of writing, all of the almost three thousand buildings were gone, including the chapel, officers club, prisoner of war buildings, and swimming pool. The water and sewer lines for a city of fifty thousand people were rusting beneath the soil. Unexploded ordnance (UXO) lay buried in many sections of the camp, including land mines, grenades, projectiles, rockets, and mortar shells. All of the wild critters had returned to their original homes to freely run the area of the camp. They joined several mules that had escaped from, or were abandoned by, the 10th Mountain Division.

After the war, Bastrop returned to a way of life similar to the way it was before war mobilization. Some sections of town still didn't have curbs, gutters, or storm drains, but the city installed a new sewer system. Few people talked about the murder of the judge's daughter, because the subject was, understandably, very painful to mention. The pain and silence continued for many years.

No mention was made in the history of Camp Swift of the murder of the judge's daughter or the execution of the soldier who was convicted of the crime, even though the incident was covered and reported by all the major newspapers in the region.

"What's the word?"

CPSIA information can be obtained
at www.ICGtesting.com
Printed in the USA
FSOW01n0107200415
6488FS